TARGET

AGATON
THE SC
YARD MYSTERY

NILS-OLOF FRANZÉN

Illustrated by Quentin Blake

TARGET

a division of
Universal-Tandem Publishing Co., Ltd.
14 Gloucester Road, London SW7 4RD

First published in Sweden by Stockholm. Alb. Bonniers Boktryckeri, 1967
and in Great Britain by André Deutsch, Ltd., 1969

First published in this edition by Universal-Tandem Publishing Co., Ltd., 1973
Second impression, 1974

ISBN 0 426 10209 6

Printed in Great Britain by The Anchor Press Ltd., and bound by Wm. Brendon & Son Ltd., both of Tiptree, Essex

Contents

Pages from Scotland Yard's *Secre*

Finn the
Forger

'Cauliflower'
Charlie

Smiling
Sandra Smith

Ernest
'Fingers' Dodge

Fat John

Hopeless
O'Donovan

'Professor'
Kalbsfleisch

Russian
Rita

The Duke of
Leicester Square

Code Register of Current Criminals*

Laughing
Willie Williams

'Hairy'
Herbert

French Jules

The Sneaker

Rosa Pasta

'Four-eyes' Harris

Dim Sven
Gustaffson

Moscow
Jim

Doctor
Doom

* *The names have been specially de-coded for this book by Agaton Sax himself*

I

Telegram from England

To you, dear reader, I must issue the following very serious warnings:

1. When you visit Scotland Yard, never mention Basement No. 3, Entrance 2B. If you do, you will probably be asked to leave immediately.
2. When you meet Inspector Arthur H. Lispington, don't ask him about certain events connected with Scotland Yard's great top secret Code Register of Current Criminals. If you do, he will be very angry indeed, and may even add your name to the Register. Then there would probably be very disagreeable consequences for you.
3. When speaking to Inspector Lispington, try, if possible, never to mention the name Goat Beard.

Now, if *you* promise to respect these three important warnings, *I* promise to tell you the whole truth about the extraordinary events which occurred in rapid succession one summer not so long ago.

It all started at five o'clock in the afternoon of Tuesday

24th August. Agaton Sax, Editor-in-Chief of the *Bykoping Post*, Sweden's smallest and best newspaper, was sitting at the window of his editorial office. Through his magnificent editorial telescope he was watching intently the big lawn-mower purchased by the Town Council the

previous year. The mower was parked outside a tobacconist's.

'Its works look as if they had seen service in the jungle,' Agaton Sax murmured angrily. 'I must write an article about this. It's a down-right scandal that Bykoping's town mower is so rusty, when the rates are so high.'

He spun his revolving chair. His super-intelligent dachshund, Tickie, who was lying at his feet, half opened her right eye to see what was going on. Agaton Sax took a blank sheet of paper, and put it into the typewriter, a wonderful invention of his own which he called the *Rapid-writer* because it worked at a terrific speed.

But hardly had he started to write, when a shrill voice was heard coming from the wall behind him.

'He's here again now! He was here last Tuesday, too!' said the wall.

'He? Who?' Agaton Sax said to the wall.

'That boy, of course! No one else was here last Tuesday, as well as today.'

'What does he want?'

'Same as usual. To deliver a telegram.'

'Send him up, will you?'

'I can't. He is already on his way,' said the wall tartly.

(The voice belonged to his Aunt Matilda, who often talked to her nephew through the speaking tube connecting the kitchen with the editorial office.)

The boy entered the room. His name was Bill, and he bowed very politely to Agaton Sax, who took the telegram and gave him a sixpence.

'This is sixpence, sir,' Bill said.

'That's right,' said Agaton Sax.

'You always give me sevenpence when Scotland Yard is involved, sir,' Bill said.

Agaton Sax looked at the telegram and nodded.

'Quite right, Bill. It is from Scotland Yard. Here's another penny. Crime does pay sometimes.'

'Thank you, sir.'

The boy disappeared, and Agaton Sax eagerly tore open the telegram.

His blue eyes narrowed into two small slits. The coded message he read was very brief—and yet Agaton Sax understood at once that he was holding in his hands one of the most important telegrams in the whole history of crime. It read as follows:

To Agaton Sax, Editor-in-Chief.

BYKOPRIMGS-PROSTEN?

X 2 PRYL Q 6 M_2 carbonate

VT-TV 1,500,000 bones.

GNITPONSIL

Agaton Sax slowly stretched out his right arm, and took down the Great Code Book from the book-case. He could, of course, decipher the telegram without any help, using system Bz 7, which he knew by heart, but he was anxious to check a few details in this extremely important message. He turned over the leaves of the Great Code Book, and then, nodding to himself, translated the mysterious text, letter by letter.

HELP! stop EXTREMELY DANGEROUS SITUATION stop SCOTLAND YARD'S SECRET CODE REGISTER OF CURRENT CRIMINALS HAS BEEN STOLEN stop THE KEY TO THE CODE STILL IN OUR HANDS stop PROBABLY SOME NEW INTERNATIONAL GANG AT WORK stop TWO HUNDRED FOREIGN DETECTIVES, INSPECTORS, POLICE CHIEFS, ETC., ARE ASSEMBLED FOR A CONFERENCE IN LONDON JUST NOW stop WE DARE NOT TELL THEM ABOUT THIS DISASTER stop I AM DESPERATE stop WHAT SHALL I DO? stop JUST IMAGINE WHAT A

STORM THERE WILL BE IF THE NEWSPAPERS GET WIND OF THIS stop PERHAPS I AM DONE FOR stop THE BRITISH GOVERNMENT ARE VERY CROSS WITH ME stop COME AT ONCE stop DON'T STOP stop HELP PLEASE!

LISPINGTON, SCOTLAND YARD

'How extraordinary,' Agaton Sax murmured, gazing thoughtfully at the flowery window curtain made by his Aunt Matilda.

Then he lit his big Tuesday pipe. (He had a different pipe for each weekday. As he solved very few problems on Sundays, he didn't have a Sunday pipe.) Within a few minutes, the room was filled with tobacco smoke, as Agaton Sax's wonderful mind worked methodically on the great mystery he now had to solve. His heart warmed as he reflected that Inspector Lispington had applied to him, Agaton Sax, for help in his great distress.

He knocked out the ashes from his pipe. All of a sudden, his small, round body seemed to grow taller. Dynamically he leaped from his chair. He was now standing in the middle of the room, his expression powerful and penetrating. Any criminal, seeing him at this moment, would have trembled in every limb and, throwing down his weapon, would have stammered: 'I give up, sir!'

'The key to the cipher,' he murmured, walking excitedly up and down the room. 'The key to the cipher is the only thing that matters. The thieves have got the Code Register, but as long as they haven't got the key, they can't read or understand it. So, their next move must be to steal the key as well. I do hope Inspector Lispington realizes that. What a terrible mess! Why didn't he call me two hours ago?'

He took out his secret note-book, jotted down a few of

his most important thoughts, and then, in a loud and commanding voice, called out to the wall:

'Aunt Matilda, ask Mrs Ericson to tidy the helicopter at once! I must leave for Gothenburg within the hour.

From there, I'll take the Super Jet Clipper to London at 19.55. The whole World Police Organization is in jeopardy.'

His dachshund, Tickie, slowly opened her right eye again. Was she, in her mind, chewing over the 1,500,000 bones mentioned in Inspector Lispington's telegram?

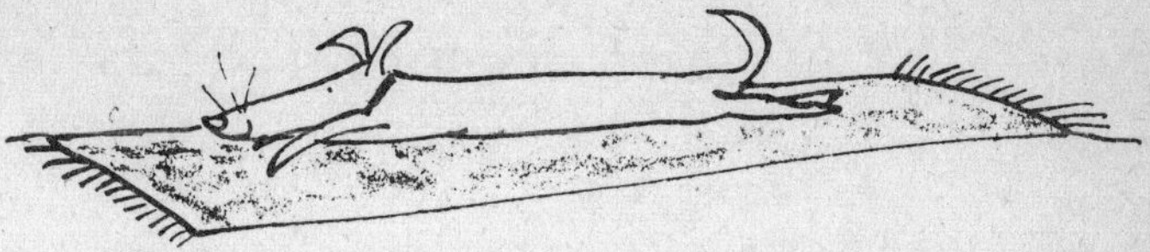

2

A warm reception

How softly the four 23,000 horse-power jet engines purred as the Super Jet Clipper headed for London above the white clouds! The speed was 500 miles per hour, or perhaps 505. The sixty-eight passengers, among them Agaton Sax, were settled comfortably in their seats, and all, except one, were unaware of the fact that among them was a man travelling on a top secret mission.

Agaton Sax had an agreement with the International Police Force permitting him to travel in disguise and on a false passport. This arrangement made it possible for him to avoid recognition by dangerous gangs, or by the police, who might delay him.

On this occasion his passport bore the photograph and the description of a very learned professor with a big moustache and long, white hair. His false name was Antonius Ams, Professor of Medieval Agriculture. He had, of course, informed Inspector Lispington about the use of this new disguise.

Agaton was lying back on his seat, dozing. Suddenly he jerked awake. Someone had touched his arm very gently. It was the stewardess, Miss Skye. She had a small silver tray in her hand.

'Are you professor Ams, sir?'

'Am I?' said Agaton Sax, who was not yet quite awake.

'Aren't you?'

'Of course I am, I am sorry, I was dreaming I was somebody else,' said Agaton Sax with a vague smile.

'I see, sir. Here is a telegram which the Captain asked me to give you.'

Agaton Sax tore open the telegram, and read the following:

ANTONIUS AMS, ABOARD THE SUPER JET CLIPPER DB 9.
PR 3 Yz 15,000,000 old shoes.
GNITPONSIL

Rapidly Agaton Sax deciphered the message:

> TWO ARMED DETECTIVES, BRICKS AND BROCKS, WILL MEET YOU AT LONDON AIRPORT stop THEY HAVE FURTHER INSTRUCTIONS FROM ME stop I AM ANXIOUSLY LOOKING FORWARD TO SEEING YOU stop THE BRITISH GOVERNMENT ARE GETTING CROSSER AND CROSSER WITH ME stop HURRY UP IF YOU CAN stop.
>
> LISPINGTON

Agaton Sax put the telegram into one of his top secret pockets, nodding to himself. Then he took out his note-book, jotted down one or two thoughts, and went back to sleep.

At 22.00 hours he landed at London Airport. Elegantly he raised his yellow straw hat to Miss Skye, before he went down the steps looking dignified and thoughtful—as befits an elderly professor of Medieval Agriculture.

Having checked through all the controls, he looked round for the two detectives. There they were! Two gentlemen dressed in black suits, and with black bowler hats which were, I'm sorry to say, green with age and much the worse for wear. In their right hands they were carrying black walking sticks.

The two detectives were watching him shrewdly, as he passed the last control point. They bowed politely to him. Doubtless, being so sharp-eyed, they had immediately realized that this medieval professor was Agaton Sax in disguise.

Agaton Sax knew he must be extremely careful, and watch his step all the time. Casually he lifted his hat, saying:

'Mr Bricks?'

'No, sir.'

'Mr Brocks?'

'Yes, sir.'

'Mr Bricks?'

'Yes, sir.'

'Good.'

'And you, sir?'

'Me?'

'Yes, sir. Who are you?'

'I am Professor Antonius Ams.'

'And whom are you looking for, sir?'

'Mr Bricks and Mr Brocks.'

'Very good, sir. And after that?'

'Inspector Lispington.'

'O.K., sir.'

Without another word the three gentlemen went to

their waiting vehicle, a splendid police car with the letters S.Y. painted in yellow on its side.

'To Inspector Lispington,' Mr Bricks ordered the driver, who saluted and then started the engine.

Mr Brocks sat with the driver, while Mr Bricks, who seemed to be of higher rank, kept Agaton Sax company. The car drove rapidly away from the airport.

Mr Bricks was a sturdy man who seemed only just able to squeeze into his shiny black suit. Agaton noted that his red hair was cropped in a rather peculiar way. Being an expert on cropped hair, he knew exactly what conclusions to draw from that. After a few minutes he decided to find out how much the two policemen really knew about the sensational case he was to investigate. He said:

'Where is the great International Police Conference being held?'

'At Scotland Yard, sir,' Mr Bricks answered.

'So it's not a secret conference?'

'By no means, sir. There's a report in the papers every day.'

'I see. Have they passed any important resolutions yet?'

'Yes, sir, indeed, sir. They have decided to use the same sized sheets of paper for all the forms that people have to fill in. The same size for all countries, that is.'

'Splendid, most interesting.'

There was a silence. They were now in north-west London, speeding through dark streets. Agaton Sax looked out of the car window.

'Have you seen Inspector Lispington lately?' he asked Mr Bricks.

'Indeed I have, sir. We'll soon be there. He's waiting for us. He'll be very happy to see you, sir, I bet.'

Two minutes later the driver stopped. He jumped out of the car, and politely opened the door for his passenger.

They were certainly in a remote part of London. Agaton Sax found himself standing in a large garden full of ancient oak trees which surrounded an octagonal house. The house had all sorts of strange bay-windows and projections, narrow balconies, and cracked flower-pots without flowers. A thick rhododendron hedge ran round the garden, and in the hedge there were many round or oval holes which had doubtless been cut out so that people of different heights—five foot two, perhaps, or six foot one—could peep out when they wanted to know what was going on in the street.

The three men walked briskly up the stone steps. Mr Bricks pulled a long, yellow, rather sad-looking piece of string hanging from a rusty nail above the door, and a bell inside rang a few notes which, strangely enough, reminded Agaton Sax of that beautiful old song *Home, sweet home . . .*

A very tall, elderly butler opened the door. For some reason or other, he carried in his right hand a hundred-year-old Kentucky rifle.

'Good evening, Benjamin,' Mr Bricks said. 'Inspector Lispington is inspecting us—I mean expecting us.'

Without a word, Benjamin the butler stepped aside, and the three gentlemen entered. Hardly had they done so, when an old suit of armour, standing near the door, toppled over and, with a crash, fell against Mr Brocks, who, completely confused, raised his hat to it. Mr Bricks glared at him, and then turned to Agaton Sax.

'Upstairs, sir,' he said.

'Hadn't you better lead the way?' Agaton Sax asked.

'Of course, sir,' said Mr Bricks, and went ahead up the stairs.

On the landing there were three massive doors. All of them seemed to be locked.

'It's the middle one we want, sir,' said Mr Bricks, and banged on it.

No answer. The three gentlemen looked at each other.

'Inspector Lispington is sometimes a bit absorbed in his crimes, if you see what I mean, sir,' said Mr Bricks, banging on the door again.

As there was still no answer, he kicked the door open with his right foot.

Mr Bricks went in first—then Agaton Sax—then Mr Brocks. As soon as they entered, things began to happen. Mr Brocks slammed the door behind them, Agaton Sax felt a pair of sinewy arms—doubtless Mr Brocks'—around his waist, and at the same time Mr Bricks turned on him, pointing a revolver at his chest.

'Ha! Caught at last, Mr Agaton Sax!' he called out in wicked triumph.

But Agaton Sax now demonstrated his extraordinary strength, agility, and perfect knowledge of ju-jitsu. With a powerful heave of his small, round body, he flung Mr Brocks in a perfect semi-circle over his right shoulder—a very elegant movement, as a matter of fact, which should have landed Mr Brocks flat on his back on the floor. But unfortunately Mr Brocks's trousers were caught by a pair of magnificent elephant tusks hanging above the door, and the result of this was that Mr Brocks, his head down, started swaying to and fro like a huge pendulum. In his first sway to the left he knocked down Mr Bricks, and in his second sway to the right he hit Agaton Sax, who lost his balance, and slipped on the newly polished floor.

All this had happened in a few seconds. Undoubtedly Agaton Sax would have been master of a dangerous situation of this fairly normal kind—but for the fact that a revolver slipped out of one of Mr Brocks' upside-down pockets. Mr Bricks made a grab at it with his right hand, caught it, and pointed it at Agaton Sax.

'All right, gentlemen, if I can call you that,' Agaton Sax said with great dignity and composure. 'You've got me cornered. You can unhook Mr Brocks, Mr Bricks. By the way, you are not Mr Bricks. You are Sycamore Flint, the infamous bank-note forger.'

Speechless with fear, the false Mr Bricks stared at Agaton Sax. 'How did you guess?' he asked at last in a half-choked voice.

'I knew it the very moment I saw your cropped hair,' Agaton Sax said. 'But unfortunately I couldn't do anything about it. And I'd be very surprised if your friend dangling up there isn't Belisarius Mock. You, Mr Mock, should thank your lucky stars that you don't weigh more than eight stone,' he added scornfully.

Swinging from left to right, (still upside-down, of course), Belisarius Mock, that is to say, the false Mr Brocks, moaned:

'Unhook me!'

'Stop fussing!' Sycamore Flint shouted at him. 'What have you got to be upset about?'

'I'm not upset—I'm upside down! I can't be hanging like this when the Boss arrives, can I?'

'Why can't you? You don't know the Boss, do you? And he doesn't know you!' Sycamore Flint retorted.

'If you don't get me down at once, I'll report you!'

'Shut up!' Sycamore Flint snarled, waving his revolver at Agaton Sax, who was listening to this exchange with the utmost attention.

'You can't behave like this to an old mate.'

'Mate! You're a useless amateur! I will get you down, but first I must bind Agaton Sax hand and foot. That's far more important than unhooking you. Turn round!' he shouted to Agaton Sax. 'Put your hands behind your back!'

Agaton Sax obeyed, but as he moved, gave him a look so penetrating that Sycamore Flint turned as white as a sheet, and a strange twitch contorted his face. He seemed at that moment to realize that his enemy's brain was working at high pressure.

This was indeed a dangerous situation, perhaps one of the most dangerous in all Agaton Sax's long and honourable career. In situations like this, one has to keep one's head, and make quick and bold decisions. Agaton Sax did not hesitate. His eyebrows beetled, his chin juttingly expressed that extraordinary will-power which inevitably leads to victory, and any onlooker would have noticed that in some strange way he managed to appear taller than his real height, towering over Sycamore Flint. (Unfortunately he cannot be compared with Belisarius Mock, on account of that gentleman's upside-down position.)

'You bully!'

'Keep quiet, I'm thinking!' Sycamore Flint shouted, scratching his cropped head. 'How can I get you down?'

'How! How?! Just unhook me! What else can you do?'

'Shut up, will you! I can't let go the revolver,' Sycamore Flint remarked.

'Then call Benjamin!'

'Good idea!' Sycamore Flint said, quite relieved; for in his heart of hearts he was not really a man who enjoyed seeing other people hanging-upside-down, caught on a pair of elephant tusks. He went to the door, called down the stairs, and listened intently. All the time Agaton Sax never took his eyes off him.

Suddenly, Sycamore Flint jerked his head, and turned to Belisarius Mock.

'Did you hear that?'

'No!'

'Shut up!'

'What?'

'Didn't you hear it?'

'What?'

'I don't know.'

'I didn't hear anything.'

'Then shut up and listen!'

Now they both heard it. A distant ticking sound—tock-tick-tock-tick-tock-tick. It sounded like a worried clock that had forgotten its rhythm and was trying hard to keep time properly. The sound came from the sofa—or rather from under the sofa, a few feet behind Agaton Sax's back.

'What is it? You're making me nervous!'

Sycamore Flint slowly turned towards Agaton Sax, and tried to transfix him with a terrifying stare—but without success.

'What is that noise?' he said in a brutal, hoarse voice. 'Answer me, you fat little man—you lying serpent!'

He saw that Agaton Sax had gone deathly pale. His long, white moustache drooped despairingly, and he stood quite motionless, as if something really terrible had happened.

'What is it?' Sycamore Flint shrieked, taking a step towards Agaton Sax. 'Answer me, you false double-dealing little traitor!'

Agaton Sax stared at him. Then, in a trembling voice, he said:

'It must be the machine.'

'What machine?' Sycamore Flint demanded.

'Yes—what machine?'

'My machine,' Agaton Sax said in a toneless voice. 'My little machine.'

'What little machine?' said Sycamore Flint, backing away.

The super-detective stared at him. His eyes were filled with terror, and the fingers of his right hand twitched nervously.

'My little infernal machine,' he said.

3

Twelve minutes to zero

'Help! Help! He's got an infernal machine! Unhook me! Quick!'

'Shut up, you coward!' stammered Sycamore Flint, his teeth chattering with fear. As he spoke he retreated a step or two, only to be hit in the back by Belisarius Mock, who just at that moment swayed violently to the left.

'Don't push me, stupid!' he shouted, breathing heavily. Then turned to Agaton Sax. 'What infernal machine are you talking about? Disconnect it, man!'

'It fell out of my pocket when you overpowered me,' Agaton Sax said. 'The clock must have started when it hit the floor.'

'Unhook me before it's too late!'

'Shut up.'

'It will go on ticking for three minutes,' Agaton Sax said. 'Then . . . then . . .'

'Then what?'

'Then . . . then . . . it's all over,' said Agaton Sax almost in a whisper.

'Quick, disconnect it, you coward!'

'I can't.'

'You can't!'

'No, I can't. My arms are pinioned.'

'What?—come here—quick—help—where am I? Here—where—where's the knife—the knife!' shrieked Sycamore Flint, starting to dig furiously in Belisarius Mock's upside-down pockets. 'Here—there—come on—be careful—give me your hands—what on earth's this?—no—that was *my* hand, not yours—I want *your* hands—not mine—quick, now I'll cut it!'

With violently trembling hands, Sycamore Flint slashed at the rope round Agaton Sax's wrists. Under the sofa, the machine was ticking inexorably. As soon as he had cut through the rope and Agaton Sax's hands were free, Sycamore Flint shot out of the room, slamming the door behind him. They heard him tumbling down the stairs in his efforts to get out of harm's way before it was too late.

'You miserable traitor—are you going to abandon me?'

Agaton Sax went down on his knees, and thrust his hand under the sofa—groping for the infernal machine. As soon as he found it, he returned to Belisarius Mock and removed the revolver from his right hand. Then he whispered in his right ear:

'Now listen very carefully, Mr Mock. The machine will explode within twelve minutes, not within three. I was lying to you just now. So you needn't be afraid to hang on for a bit. But you must not say one single word, do you understand? Whatever I do, you must keep absolutely silent.'

Stupid with fear, Belisarius Mock nodded his upside-down head violently. Agaton Sax tiptoed to the door, and opened it cautiously. Everything was quiet, except for a strange sound coming from downstairs. Perhaps it was Sycamore Flint's teeth—still chattering.

One of the most extraordinary faculties Agaton Sax possessed, was the uncanny skill he had for imitating other people's voices. Now he called down the stairs in a voice which was so like Belisarius Mock's that even Mock's own mother would have sworn it was her son's:

'Come up, Sycamore! I have unhooked myself. I've got our fat little friend under control, and I've disconnected the infernal machine!'

'Fine! Excellent!' called back Sycamore Flint. 'I'll come at once!'

They heard his heavy steps on the stairs. Agaton Sax stood just behind the door. In silent terror Belisarius Mock watched this strange man who had imitated his own hoarse voice. Sycamore Flint stopped outside the half-open door. He was breathing heavily.

'Are you there, Belisarius?'

'Yes, of course I am here! Come in, everything's O.K.,' said Agaton Sax in his borrowed voice.

The door was pushed open, very slowly, and Agaton Sax saw Sycamore Flint's right hand. He was pointing a revolver into the room, just to be on the safe side.

'Ah!' Sycamore Flint cried, as Agaton Sax pounced, wrenched the revolver out of his hand, and pulled him into the room. The attack was so violent and so sudden that the astonished Sycamore nearly lost his balance, and went skidding across the highly polished floor. Panting, he stared into the muzzle of the revolver, now pointing menacingly at him.

'The game is up, my dear Sycamore Flint,' said Agaton

Sax in a calm, firm voice, shutting the door behind his guest. ‘That’s that. You have a lot to learn,’ he added scornfully.

‘The infernal machine,’ said Sycamore Flint, his vocal chords trembling. ‘Is it . . . ?’

‘Be quiet. I’ve found it, but I can’t stop it.’

‘You . . . can’t . . . stop it?’

‘No, it will go on ticking until . . .’

‘Help! Unhook me!’

‘Until . . ? But then . . ?’

‘Yes, of course!’

‘But . . . if . . . how . . ?’

‘We’ve only ten minutes left,’ said Agaton Sax. ‘It will take me two minutes to tie your hands, one minute to unhook Belisarius Mock, two minutes to bind him, two minutes to tie Benjamin the butler’s hands, three minutes to lock you all up. Call Benjamin up here immediately. He must bring me two yards of rope, but tell him to leave his rifle downstairs, if you don’t mind!’

Sycamore Flint obeyed like a sleep-walker. The silent Benjamin came up, took in the situation at a glance, turned pale and surrendered. Together they unhooked Belisarius Mock, who wiped his forehead with a trembling hand.

‘When you are up, you are up, and when you are down, you are down,’ said Agaton Sax, sitting down calmly, as if there was no hurry at all. He had put the little black box, which was hardly bigger than a match-box, on the table. The three men lined up in front of him, their faces ashen. One by one he tied their hands behind their backs.

‘Excellent,’ he murmured to himself. ‘Just relax, gentlemen, and no harm will befall you. Are you ready to follow me? Fine! Now let us all go down to the basement.'

He picked up the little black box, which was now ticking loudly again, and the four men walked down the stairs. The basement was a warren of small rooms, probably used as guest-chambers where the gang could lock up their innocent victims.

'This way, please,' Agaton Sax said very politely, gently pushing Belisarius Mock into one of these dark rooms. He shut the door and then locked it carefully. After that, it was Benjamin the butler's turn.

'And now Sycamore Flint,' Agaton Sax said grimly, 'I want to know what you are doing in this house?'

'Me, sir? I can't say, sir.'

'You can't? Then I will tell you. You are expecting a visitor. What time is he due to arrive?'

Sycamore Flint heaved a deep sigh.

'At midnight, sir.'

'And who is he?'

'I don't know, sir. I swear I don't!'

'Don't lie to me, Sycamore Flint! Remember—I am Agaton Sax!'

'I never lie, sir—Sir Agaton, I mean. I swear!'

'I understand,' Agaton Sax said in a menacing voice, slowly turning the little box between his thumb and his forefinger. 'All right. You don't know him. But you must know why he is coming here.'

'No, Sir Agaton! No—yes, I mean! He'll give me something.'

'Give you something? What?'

'I don't know, Sir Agaton! I swear!'

'And what will you do with whatever it is he gives you?'

'I'll give it away.'

'To whom?'

'That I don't know, Sir Agaton, I swear!'

'Does this man know you?'

'No, nobody knows anybody else.'

'I see. But you know me now, don't you? So you had better tell me the whole truth.'

'Yes, indeed, Sir Agaton. The Boss ordered me to be here. The unknown man I told you about just now is coming here, and he'll give me something and tell me who to pass it on to.'

'Very good. You are improving, Sycamore Flint. And who is the Boss?'

'I wish I knew, Sir Agaton—but I don't, I swear.'

'You don't know? Remember—I am Agaton Sax!'

'I swear, Sir Agaton—your lordship, I mean, sir! I swear. It's a secret.'

'A secret? But you just said that the Boss ordered you to come here! So you must have met the Boss?'

'No, your lordship, somebody phoned me.'

'Who phoned you?'

'The Boss—he said he was the Boss.'

'But then you must have recognised his voice?'

'No, your lordship, his voice is secret too.'

'Come now, Sycamore Flint! Remember my infernal machine!'

The poor man was trembling in every limb. 'He must be telling the truth,' Agaton Sax reflected. 'He's as soft as a soft-boiled egg.'

'Let us get on, Sycamore Flint,' Agaton Sax continued.

'How were you and your friend Belisarius Mock able to impersonate the detectives Bricks and Brocks?'

'We had orders to get the genuine Bricks and Brocks out of the way. So we did. We captured them and locked them up. They are now at 119 Sloane Street, second floor, first door on the left. They're all right there. Very comfortable, your lordship. I wouldn't mind being there myself just now, your lordship, if you understand what I mean, sir.'

'And how did you know that I was travelling as Professor Ams?'

'The Boss told me on the telephone, your lordship.'

'And what were you to do with me when you had taken me prisoner?'

'We were to take you to the Boss.'

'And where's that?'

'That he didn't say, your lordship. The unknown man I was waiting for was to tell me that.'

'And the password?'

'The password, your lordship?'

'Yes. Since you don't know the unknown man, and he doesn't know you, he must surely give you a password when he arrives?'

'Oh yes, certainly, your lordship! I'm so sorry. I do apologise, your lordship. I am to say: *What station?*'

'And he?'

'He must answer: *Next stop, Braxington!*'

'And what is your secret name, Sycamore Flint?'

'It's S. F. Seventeen.'

'And the other man's secret name?'

'D. G. Twelve.'

'Anything else you would like to tell me?'

'No, your lordship. I swear I don't know any more.'

'Very good. I have finished with you for the moment. Will you please step inside?'

He locked the door of Sycamore Flint's cell and glanced at his watch, then said in a loud voice:

'Listen carefully, gentlemen! The infernal machine is now disconnected. The time device will no longer explode

it. But I warn you, this infernal machine is super-sensitive to noise, however slight or feeble it may be. If any noise at all comes from these guest rooms where you are all so comfortably accommodated, the machine will explode immediately. Good day, gentlemen!'

With an elegant gesture he brushed the dust off his hat. Then he adjusted his false moustache, and went up the stairs. As he was crossing the hall, he saw a big waste-paper basket near the door. He dropped the little black box nonchalantly into it. The little black box was absolutely empty. It had been empty all the time. It contained no infernal machine and never had. Its deadly ticking had in fact been produced by Agaton Sax himself, who, as you know, is an extremely skilful imitator, mimic and ventriloquist. So skilful, in fact, that he can even make a ticking noise that seems to come from a little black box which contains no infernal machine.

4

Password to headquarters

How wonderfully quiet the house was, now that the three troublesome rogues were too scared to make a sound!

Who was the owner of the house? Of course it did not belong to Inspector Lispington at all, he had never lived here. No, doubtless it was the home of some sly and treacherous criminal who was a member of this dangerous gang.

Agaton Sax sat down at a table in the living-room. His mind ranged methodically over the events of the past few hours. The more he reflected, the more he became convinced that an enormously clever criminal was behind all that had happened. A real master in the world of crime, with a brain of stupendous quality—an utterly unscrupulous man, who had never been outwitted and who could, probably, be caught only by Agaton Sax himself. This man, whoever he might be, was in possession of three vital facts:

1. That Scotland Yard had sent for Agaton Sax.
2. That Agaton Sax was travelling as Professor Ams.

3. That the genuine detectives, Bricks and Brocks, had been ordered to meet Agaton Sax at the airport.

With a start Agaton Sax jumped up, went over to the telephone and dialled Scotland Yard.

'Can I speak to the superintendent in charge, please?'

'What about?'

'Crime.'

'What sort of crime?'

'What's that got to do with you? This is Agaton Sax speaking, and I am in a hurry.'

'I've never heard of you, and you had better tell me what crime you want to report, or I'll report *you*.'

'Very good. You can do that later. But first take down this message. Two of your detectives, Bricks and Brocks, are locked up at 119 Sloane Street, second floor, first door on the left. Have you got that? Good. Send someone there to pick them up. That's all for tonight. Further instructions will follow tomorrow.'

'Wait a minute! Don't hang up! Who are you? Mr Slacks, did you say? Or was it Snacks? Hallo! Hallo!'

'Good night.'

Agaton Sax hung up the receiver. Then he went outside and moved the car to the back of the house. When he returned to the room, he switched off all the lights except one, for his brain worked much more efficiently in semi-darkness. The gang which had just failed to catch him, he thought, must be the same one that had stolen Scotland Yard's Secret Code Register of Current Criminals. Evidently the leader of this gang—the Boss—was a very efficient man. The members of the gang did not know each other, with the exception of the three men Agaton Sax had captured, who obviously did. Agaton Sax was fully convinced that no one knew the Boss, whereas the Boss knew everyone. Thanks to this cunning arrangement the Boss could act anonymously, keeping everyone in the dark, so that he was increasingly respected, even feared, by all his subordinates, who trembled even at his name, although it wasn't his real name, anyway, since nobody knew that.

The night was dark. There had been a little pale moonlight a few moments ago, but even that had gone now. The outlines of the huge oak trees stirred in the breeze. Their great, twisted branches moved like dark, threatening arms against the windows. Far away, an owl's sinister hooting cut through the silence.

Agaton Sax glanced at his bullet-proof watch. It was exactly 23.45. He stretched his legs, and lit his last Tuesday pipe.

Suddenly there was a tapping against the wall. Slowly he turned his head towards the window and listened intently. Was there a face half-hidden behind one of those branches?

He rose stealthily from the chair, tip-toed to the wall, followed it till he reached the window, and cautiously peered out between the curtains. Another low sound came from outside—like someone knocking very gently on the window-pane.

He strained his eyes till they ached, trying to see if there really was someone there knocking on the window. At last he thought he saw the leaves move in the darkness, as if a thousand fingers were groping for the window-fasteners.

'Nonsense,' he murmured, and pulled himself together. 'It's only the branches.'

This had been a moment's weakness. Now he was his old self again, supremely calm, and prepared to fight anyone. He puffed at his pipe, and jotted down a couple of important thoughts in his secret note-book.

As he was shutting the little book, he heard a noise coming from the street. This time there was no doubt about it. A car was approaching in the darkness. Now it was slowing down. As it stopped, the beam of the headlights suddenly silhouetted the seven-hundred-year old oak tree outside the window.

Agaton Sax remained seated; completely calm, but keeping a sharp eye on the window. The car's engine stopped, the lights were switched off, and then there was a deep silence, which lasted only a few seconds. A man Agaton Sax had never seen before was approaching the house, the gravel crunching under his heavy feet.

Agaton Sax did not move. He was waiting. The man walked up the stone steps. He pulled at the yellow, forlorn-looking piece of string, and the bell rang. As the brief clanging died away into silence, Agaton Sax rose from his chair.

With a firm step he walked to the door. It seemed as if the two men were waiting for each other on each side of it. After a moment's pause, Agaton Sax said in a low mysterious voice:

'What station?'

'Next stop Braxington.'

'Your name?'

'D. G. Twelve. And yours?'

'S. F. Seventeen. You can come in.'

Agaton Sax opened the door. A very thin man, wearing a blue trench-coat and a grey-green checked cap, was standing on the door-step, a burnt-out cigarette between his lips. The man nodded, then, with a respectful salute, walked in, shaking the rain-drops from his cap. Agaton Sax looked him over from head to foot and noted that his eyes were watery blue.

The stranger gave an apologetic shrug and spoke: 'Of heard this have never I street before, it so some took me time afraid I'm the house find to. Excuse hope, sir, you'll I me, late two being minutes for.'

Agaton Sax was inwardly amazed by this mysterious speech. The stranger had spoken in such a natural voice that for a moment, he wondered whether suddenly he had begun to hear things backwards, or whether the stranger was indeed completely incoherent. However, Agaton Sax is an accomplished master of the noble art of self-control. He is also a world-renowned linguist, fluent in more than fourteen languages. So he found it very easy to translate the stranger's words quickly. They simply meant: 'I have never heard of this street before, so I'm afraid it took me some time to find the house. I hope you'll excuse me, sir, for being two minutes late.'

In the most natural of voices, as if he had never spoken any other language, Agaton Sax answered:

'Man old, worry don't. Yourself home at make just, business and talk we'll.'

'Sir, you thank! Up my hang won't I coat, must for I once at off be.'

'Course of, understand I.'

Agaton Sax had wondered earlier why the stranger

called him 'sir', but he concealed his surprise, and went on:

'Message have the secret you you with?'

'Speak just can I plain now common English, sir?'

'Yes, you can.'

'Thanks a lot, sir. You see, this double-talk is dreadfully confusing, my head gets in a whirl when I have to speak it, and I don't know if I've finished when I've started, or started when I've finished, if you see what I mean. But as you know, this is the way the Boss wants it, and it's not for me to disobey.'

He was digging deep down in the pockets of his trench-coat, and at last fished out a grey-yellow envelope. Agaton Sax thought it would be wise to put the stranger's honesty to a final test. He looked at him enquiringly and said:

'Know if do you Belisarius Flint Sycamore and Mock caught have Ams Professor Antonius, Airport who at tonight London arrived?'

The stranger looked at him reproachfully with his watery blue eyes. Then he took the cigarette out of his mouth, and said in an almost sad voice:

'Speak you really must talk-double time the all? What Basalarius and Kicksamore Antimonius Shrink talking you are, sir, of? Sir, sorry I'm, very but not I'm languages at clever, see you.'

'Yes, see I,' Agaton Sax said, giving the man a kindly pat on the shoulder. 'Very good D.G. Twelve. Now give me that letter.'

He opened the grey-yellow envelope and glanced quickly at the contents. Then he murmured:

'Excellent. Where are you going now D.G. Twelve?'

'To my convertible sofa bed. Tired very am I—I'm sorry, I mean I'm very tired, sir.'

'Good. But first I'll show you something.'

'Show me something, sir?'

'Yes. Will you please follow me?'

Agaton Sax led the way to the basement. They stopped outside the room where Belisarius Mock was locked up.

'Hallo, Belisarius Mock! Are you there? Can you hear me?'

'Yes, indeed, sir.'

'Then listen very carefully. Move right across to the back of the room.'

'Yes, sir. I'm going. I can't go any further now, sir. The wall is in my way, sir. It's banging my forehead, sir. Do you want me to press on all the same, sir?'

'No, don't. Just stay where you are Belisarius Mock. Now, D.G. Twelve, I'll show you something really interesting. Come here!'

He opened the door, beckoned D.G. Twelve to come closer and told him to peep through the doorway. D.G. Twelve obeyed without hesitation. Agaton Sax pounced on his victim and pushed him into the room. He locked the door, and then ran up the stairs. Seated at a magnificent writing-desk in one of the inner rooms, he read the letter once again. It ran:

Order from the Boss to S.F. Seventeen.

Watch Agaton Sax's every move until I send three relief guards along. Mock, Benjamin and D.G. Twelve must keep watch over him with two revolvers each. Do not trust him for one single second. He is extremely dangerous. When you have been relieved go to 13B Paddington

Road. Somebody will be expecting you there at 03.00 hours.

Agaton Sax thought hard. He must decide at once what to do next. What was 13B Paddington Road? Was it the gang's Headquarters, where the Boss, like a spider in the centre of its web, wove together all the threads of the various crimes he planned and committed? Or was it just one of the many houses to which the members of the gang were sent to receive new orders? Nobody could know for certain—not even Agaton Sax. But he realised that he had no choice but to set off at once for Paddington Road.

Being a man who acted quickly on any decision he stood up at once, putting the letter into one of his secret pockets. Two minutes later he was no longer an absent-minded professor of Medieval Agriculture, but was sitting at the wheel of D.G. Twelve's car, driving fast. As he left the octagonal house he had grabbed his suitcase from the car which had met him at the airport, changed into golfing clothes, peeled off his drooping moustache, and was restored to his normal spruce appearance.

He also carried a solid walking-stick, in the upper end of which he had installed a small tear-gas revolver. This was one of his own ingenious inventions and he always packed it in a suit-case when he went abroad.

5

Orders from an unseen boss

13B Paddington Road proved to be one of the many millions of innocent looking houses which cannot possibly arouse the suspicions of Scotland Yard or the International Police Force. A narrow flight of steps led up to a very pleasant-looking green door.

It appeared to be the only house in a neighbourhood dominated by office-blocks. That would certainly be an advantage to criminal gangs, or indeed anyone with a reason to dread the daylight, for at night the street was absolutely dark and empty.

With his usual perspicacity Agaton Sax assumed that he could very easily penetrate this centre of crime disguised as one of the gang, since all the criminal activities directed by the Boss were based on the principle that no member of his gang should know any other member, and that the Boss himself should be anonymous and unseen.

In all these assumptions Agaton Sax was quite right. As soon as he rang the door bell, a grating, raucous voice answered from inside:

'What station?'

'Next stop Braxington!'

'Come in.' The voice croaked hoarsely from behind the green door. At the same time the door opened, and Agaton Sax found himself facing a man wearing dark glasses. Without saying a word the man let Agaton Sax pass straight into the hall. Once inside he looked around. The room was in semi-darkness. Along the walls four men were sitting on spindly wooden chairs. They were reading comic strips, and none took any notice of Agaton Sax's arrival, they didn't even lift their eyes from their papers. They were dressed in a great variety of clothes. One of them, who was chewing all the time—probably gum—was dressed in a black jacket, grey-striped trousers and very elegant black shoes. Another was wearing an enormous Icelandic sweater, and had a fishing-net fastened to his belt. The third seemed to be a bicycle repairer, for he had a large oil-can at his feet and eleven spanners of various sizes on his lap. The fourth man was dressed as a policeman, from which Agaton Sax immediately deduced that he was most unlikely to be one.

'These disguises are very interesting indeed,' he thought to himself as he sat down on an empty chair. The man who had opened the door disappeared into another room. Agaton Sax took up a newspaper which was lying on the floor, but hardly had he opened it, when a powerful voice was heard:

'Eleven B is Under-Boss this speaking. Q Nine yet returned has?'

'Am sir, here, yes I.'

The mysterious voice had come from a picture hanging on the wall. The picture represented a Mexican, or, perhaps, a Nicaraguan, cactus, and it did not take

Agaton Sax long to realise that behind the cactus there was a loud-speaker. But whose voice was it? Doubtless the man was in an adjacent room, and was speaking into a microphone.

'Good very. Go Q Nine you can. Nine o'clock at morning morrow-to be in must Buddenham Place you instructions further for.'

'Right, sir—sorry, I mean : sir, right.'

Q Nine was the bicycle repairer. He bowed to the cactus and went away to snatch a few hours' sleep.

There was silence—broken only by the clatter of the elegantly dressed gentleman's monocle, which slipped from his right eye and fell to the ground, as he suddenly nodded asleep.

Nothing more happened for a long time. It was now three o'clock. Agaton Sax yawned discreetly. There was a ring at the door, and a heavy weight champion wrestler came in, and immediately disappeared.

Ten minutes later a voice spoke from the cactus again—but now it was a different voice, curt, abrupt, and peremptory. The four men waiting in the hall jerked awake as the voice said :

'Speaking is the Boss this. Arrived yet S.F. Seventeen has?'

Agaton Sax, who, you remember, was now impersonating S.F. Seventeen, answered at once, in a perfect imitation of that gentleman's voice.

'Over I hour an arrived, sir, ago.'

'Locked your up have prisoner you?'

'Indeed I, sir, have. Under, sir, everything control is.'

'Good,' said the cold, imperious voice from behind the cactus. 'You can speak ordinary English now. You do realise how important your prisoner really is, don't you?'

'Sir?'

'Agaton Sax is the ace of detectives. You know his reputation, S.F. Seventeen?'

'I do indeed, sir. Very much so.'

'Then you understand why I had to do what I did tonight. How many men did you leave on guard?'

'Three, sir.'

'That won't be enough, he's dangerous and clever. I'll send over another three in the morning. Six seems more appropriate to guard a man of Agaton Sax's powers.'

'I understand, sir,' Agaton Sax said with a secret smile. 'Do you want me to go back to the house and check that everything is all right, sir?'

'No, that is not necessary. You stay here. I have a very important mission for you. But first, you can take five hours sleep. You had eight hours last night according to my secret note-book. Is that correct?'

'Yes, sir.'

'Good. When you have had your five hours rest, go to Scotland Yard.'

'To Scotland Yard, sir?' Agaton Sax managed to sound really frightened. 'Must I really, sir . . ?'

'Don't interrupt. Take the green four-seater Morris with the bullet-proof windows and tyres. Drive to Scotland Yard, then park outside at exactly ten o'clock. Stay in the car, reading a newspaper called *The Scottish Pastor's Sunday News*—you'll find it on the back seat. You will be disguised as a temporary secretary on the staff of the Brosnian Embassy. You'll wear steel-rimmed spectacles, and smoke a pipe. Above all you must appear calm and relaxed. If anybody asks your name, it is Bartolo Paragotta. Is that clear?'

'Perfectly, sir.'

'Very good. At 10.15 things will begin to move. A man will come out of Scotland Yard's main entrance. He'll be wearing a grey overcoat and a black hat, and be carrying a large pigskin briefcase with a brass catch, in his right hand. He'll nod politely to the guards and then walk briskly up to your car. This man is Old Goat Beard.'

'Old Goat Beard, sir?' Agaton Sax exclaimed genuinely astonished—for once he didn't need to hide his feelings.

'Yes. This man is none other than Kossoparamonescono, Brosnian Chief of Police. He's seventy and he wears a black goatee. That's why he's nicknamed Old Goat Beard.'

'Of course! How silly of me not to think of it myself,' Agaton Sax said, making a little bow in the direction of the cactus.

'Quite! As I said just now, he'll make straight for your car—or, rather, that's what you'll think he's doing. Actually he'll pass you and get in a taxi waiting for him a few yards further on. The taxi will drive off at once, and you will follow round Trafalgar Square to St. Martin's-in-the-Fields, where you'll both stop. Kossoparamonescono, or Old Goat Beard, will get out of his car and look round for a moment or two. Now, leave your car, walk up to him, lift your hat and say with a smile: "Chief of Police, Kossoparamonescono, I presume?" He will answer, "yes," and you must reply, "Bartolo Paragotta from the Brosnian Embassy, at your service, your Excellency. I have orders to drive your Excellency to the Brosnian Embassy, where the Ambassador is expecting you for lunch." Old Goat Beard will thank you and get into your car. Then drive him straight here to me at 13B Paddington Road. Is that clear?'

'Yes, sir. But what shall I do if he notices that we are *not* driving to the Brosnian Embassy, as I told him?'

'Trust me, he won't notice.'

'Very good, sir.'

'Now repeat the whole plan, so that I can be sure you remember the details.'

Agaton Sax repeated what he had been told. When he had finished, the Boss said—and there was almost a hint of humanity in his icy voice:

'Excellent. I'll make a note that you are to get a pay rise of two and six a week. Now go and get some sleep.'

'Thank you, sir.'

Agaton Sax turned away and walked calmly to the door. The four rogues were still half asleep on their chairs. As he came out into the street, the first thing he saw was a green four-seater Morris. He got in and drove straight to the Hotel Splendide, where he went up to his room and put through a phone call.

'Hallo! Is that you, Inspector Lispington?'

'Good night,' came the sleepy and confused reply. 'I'm sorry, I mean good morning—no, I mean hallo!'

'Is that Inspector Lispington speaking?'

'Is it? No, you must be mistaken. I am Inspector Lispington. Do you wish to speak to me? Who is it?'

'It's me, Agaton Sax.'

There was a pause. Then Agaton Sax heard Lispington's voice, very faint, very far away:

'Are you . . . Have you . . ?'

'Don't worry, Lispington. Everything is O.K. Any news? What are the British Government saying?'

'They are getting crosser and crosser,' Lispington said sadly. 'What's happened to you? Where are you? Were you kidnapped? Have you got on to the scent yet?'

'Yes, you can rely on me, everything will be all right,' Agaton Sax said kindly. 'I'll tell you all the details later.'

'But I must see you now!' Lispington exclaimed. 'The International Police Conference starts a new session to-morrow. You know what will happen within the next two days. They will want to see the great Register of Current Criminals—the famous Register known to every detective in Europe—our pride—the most secret of all secret weapons in our ceaseless struggle against crime. It's gone—stolen! And I promised them!'

'What did you promise them?' asked Agaton Sax, very much alarmed.

'When I sent out the invitation cards for the International Police Conference, I promised all the delegates I would show them the Secret Register! They are all waiting for the solemn moment when I take them down to the basement . . . How dreadful! I can't tell them it's been stolen, can I? Perhaps I can tell them I have lent it to someone. Perhaps I can say that I had to send it off to be re-bound?'

'Why?'

'Why? What do you mean, why?'

'I mean—why should you have chosen this moment to send it away for re-binding?'

'I don't know. I really don't know, Agaton Sax.'

'I'm sorry, Lispington, but I don't know either.'

'Then there's no hope. I'm done for as I told you right from the start.'

'Wait a minute. Perhaps you could tell them that you have lent the Register to me, Agaton Sax.'

'But you haven't got it! How could I explain that you have not given it back to me? I can't say that you have disappeared with it, can I?'

'No, you can't. That would not be true. But tell me—how much longer does the Conference last?'

'Another four days.'

'Listen carefully, Lispington. You will have the Register back within three days. That I promise you. Until then—keep the Conference busy. Organise dinner-parties and excursions for them. Arrange as many lectures as possible. Show them your files, set up Committees, sub-committees, working-parties, and *ad hoc* study groups, anything you can think of. Now I must sleep. Can I see you at Scotland Yard tomorrow morning at half past eight?'

'Yes, please do!'

'Very well. Then I can tell you what has happened so far, and you can tell me all about the Register.'

'Will anything else happen to-night?' Lispington asked quaveringly.

'Probably not to-night. Something may tomorrow morning. Just one other thing before I hang up—tell your people to send a few men to 5 Bob Street. It's just a few doors from the main road. Your men should be there at eight tomorrow morning, that's in about four hours. They'll have a fine haul, I promise you. That's all for to-night. Good night, Lispington.'

Agaton Sax replaced the receiver wearily. He had had a very tiring day. Three minutes later he was asleep.

6

Conference at Scotland Yard

Agaton Sax wore no disguise as he drove to Scotland Yard the following morning. With a firm step he hurried along the familiar corridors, and entered Inspector Lispington's office at 8.30 sharp.

Lispington was standing at the window, wringing his hands in despair. Agaton Sax coughed slightly. Lispington spun round, colour flooded his cheeks; he seemed suddenly to be fired with new hope and confidence. He almost ran to Agaton Sax, and clasped both his hands.

'It's good to see you, Agaton Sax!' he exclaimed. 'I was terribly distressed when I heard that you had been kidnapped.'

'Are Bricks and Brocks O.K.?'

'Yes, indeed. Sit down and let me explain what happened. Bricks and Brocks drove out to the airport to meet you. As they turned into Pudney Road, which is a dark lane, they saw two men working in a large hole in the middle of the street, so they were forced to stop the car. Bricks got out to have a look at the hole and see if it would be possible for the car to pass. As he did so someone pushed him into it. Mr Brocks leapt out of the car to find out why on earth his colleague was inspecting the bottom of the hole; someone else—or perhaps the same man—pushed Mr Brocks into the hole too. After that it was easy for the rogues to keep them out of the way. The rest you know better than I do.'

'Yes,' said Agaton Sax, thoughtfully pulling at his elegant moustache. 'I do know the rest. But tell me, Lispington, what exactly are the contents of the Secret Code Register of Current Criminals? I mean, what special information does it contain? And how did the gang manage to steal it?'

Inspector Lispington heaved a deep sigh and sank further into his arm-chair.

'The Secret Code Register contains the names of several thousand international criminals, with descriptions, photographs, finger-prints, and so on, together with a very detailed list of all the crimes they are known to have committed. Even the names of several unknown criminals and their unknown crimes can be found in the Register.'

'Unknown?'

'Yes. Undiscovered crimes and criminals that we don't know about yet although they must exist.'

'I understand.'

'Of course the Register is absolutely top-secret.' Lispington continued. 'It's disappearance is nothing less than a disaster. Hundreds of criminals operating in various countries could now be warned by the thieves, but fortunately . . .'

'Fortunately what?' Agaton Sax said.

'Fortunately the Register is written in code, as you

know. That means, of course, that nobody can read it without having the Key to the code. The Key is in a small book, about 24 pages long, containing all the tables and formulae you need to read the Register.'

'And where's the Key now?'

'It is here in Scotland Yard, well locked up. We always keep our keys under lock and key, you see.'

'I see.'

Nodding thoughtfully Agaton Sax stood up. 'So at this moment there is no one in the whole world who can read the Register? You in Scotland Yard can't read it, for you only have the Key and not the Register. The thieves can't read it, for they only have the Register and not the Key. Is that correct?'

'Yes, that's correct,' said Lispington with a nod. 'That is what I have been trying to tell the British Government, but all they do is get crosser and crosser.'

Agaton Sax paced slowly up and down, his hands behind his back. After a while he stopped, looked at Lispington, and said:

'How did it happen?'

'Four men in white uniforms came to Scotland Yard early in the morning in a van, and collected the Register.'

'Collected it?'

'They said they came from *Wash Whiteman's Laundries*, and this seemed to be perfectly all right, because their van had *Wash Whiteman's Laundries Wash White Whiter* painted on the side. As they said they had come to collect the laundry, the guards let them in. What happened next is not quite clear, but we do know that a few minutes later they carried out the fourteen wooden boxes in which the Code Register was kept. The guards helped them to lift the boxes into the van. A moment later the van and the men were gone.'

Inspector Lispington closed his eyes and wiped his forehead. Agaton Sax patted him on the shoulder.

'Again will all be right everything,' he said hoarsely.

'What did you say?' Lispington exclaimed.

'Everything will be all right again, I mean.'

'My dear Agaton Sax, how you frightened me! I had a sudden feeling you were speaking backwards. I'm sorry. I'm so upset and so nervous.'

'Listen, Lispington. Tell me about Kossoparamonescono.'

'Kossoparamonescono?' Lispington said, a pale smile lighting up his long face. 'Kossoparamonescono is the life and soul of the International Police Conference. Everybody likes him. You see he manages to create an atmosphere of good will wherever he goes. He is the Brosnian Chief of Police, but an extremely nice chap in spite of that. I hope you will have an opportunity of meeting him. You speak Brosnian if I remember rightly.'

'Yes. Now, could you take me down to the basement where the thieves stole the Register?'

They went down to Basement No. 3. They passed through long, dark corridors, and at last arrived at Entrance 2B. The door was so low that they had to stoop to go through to the little room. Above the door there was a notice saying:

MIND YOUR HEAD

'Behind that door we keep the Key to the Register,' Lispington whispered, pointing to another door, which was hardly visible in the darkness. 'The Key is kept locked up in a small metal box.'

Agaton Sax nodded, glancing at the door with interest.

'And here,' Lispington continued, still whispering, is where we kept the fourteen volumes of the Register.'

Agaton Sax did not answer. For a while he stood in silence, obviously weighing up everything he had been told, and a lot more besides. At last he said :

'There is no doubt that this crime was planned by one of the real master minds of the underworld. Any man capable of perpetrating a crime of this magnitude must have a really ruthless and subtle mind—I think he will prove more dangerous than any other crook I've ever encountered.'

'Oh dear !' Lispington muttered miserably.

'As far as I can make out,' Agaton Sax went on, as the two men walked slowly back to Lispington's office, 'we are up against the same enigmatic mind that baffled you at every stage in the case of the blue oranges.'

'Do you really think so? Oh dear !' Lispington sighed, remembering painfully a most unhappy episode in his early career.

'Yes. Everything seems to indicate that it's the same man. And if it is—then it's also the man who stole the Duchess of Suffolk's eighteen diamonds, and smuggled them out of the country in a coconut. You will recall that you finally found the two halves of the nut near the border between France and Belgium. I am afraid you've got the same hard nut to crack.'

Lispington heaved another deep sigh.

'And this man,' Agaton Sax continued purposefully, 'is certainly the man who, only five years ago, was secretary to ISWS (International Society for Wholesale Smuggling). He has had an extraordinary career. Only a year after leaving the Smugglers he was appointed vice-president of MCCL (Mink Coat Collectors Limited). Hundreds of Mink coats came into their possession as you can well imagine. Fifteen months later, he was president of BNFC (Bank Note Forgery Company), which printed some twelve million pound notes. Shortly after that he was appointed Managing Director of QMSL (Quick Master-Strokes Limited).'

'And now?' Lispington asked breathlessly.

'Now you can see for yourself. Now he commands the whole World of Crime—or rather he will, as soon as he can read your Code Register. Then he will know as much as you know, or knew, about known and unknown criminals and crimes. He will be able to exploit his unique knowledge recklessly, because it will be in his power to forestall every move. With the Register, he can threaten, command, blackmail and subdue all his competitors. Indeed, never in the history of Crime has one single man been invested with so much power, nor had so many chances for breaking the law for his own gain! Lispington—Disaster lies ahead!'

Agaton Sax had worked himself into such a frenzy that he could no longer contain his excitement. He leapt up and paced the room, not even noticing Lispington, who seemed about to faint.

'But you forget that he . . .'

'That he what?'

'That he has not got the Key to the Register,' Lispington gasped.

'That's true. But that's no excuse for underestimating

his subtlety,' Agaton Sax warned his colleague. 'However, don't worry, everything will come right. I, Agaton Sax, have an even greater intellect! How foolish of him to think that he can get the better of me!'

'Have you found new clues then?' asked Lispington, hope creeping into his voice.

'Yes, many,' Agaton Sax said. 'As a matter of fact,' he confided suddenly, 'I'm already on his track!'

'What? Tell me all about it!' Lispington breathed. Agaton Sax slowly twirled his elegant moustache, then went on seriously:

'Listen carefully, Lispington. You know you can trust me. I shall shortly have a meeting with one of the delegates of the International Police Conference.'

'What! With a Chief of Police or a Superintendent behind my back?' Lispington exclaimed, almost angry.

'Please don't get excited, Lispington. I'm not doing anything behind your back, since I'm telling you all about it now. But you see, I simply must talk to one of the delegates. It won't take more than ten minutes, and I'll keep you scrupulously informed of all that happens.'

Agaton Sax now gave Lispington a brief account of all that had happened to him since his arrival in London. The only thing he did not mention was that he would be seeing Police Chief Kossoparamonescono in a few minutes. Instead he walked to the door, muttering a brief apology for having to hurry off.

'I understand,' Lispington said, with another deep sigh. He rose from his chair. I suppose I'd better call the Government. But he did no such thing. Instead he sank heavily into his chair, which sagged so dejectedly under his weight that it rather resembled its unhappy occupant.

'See you later,' he murmured, with a vague wave of his left hand.

Agaton Sax walked slowly out of the huge building. In a few minutes he would face one of the most difficult tasks in his remarkable career.

7

Enter Old Goat Beard. Exit the Key

From Scotland Yard Agaton Sax went straight to his hotel, where he changed his clothes. He slipped out of the hotel's back-door and drove along Victoria Street until he was almost at Scotland Yard. He turned into a small, quiet street, which faced the entrance to the building. He parked his car but didn't get out. Following the orders he had received from the Boss, he picked up the copy of *The Scottish Pastor's Sunday News* from the back seat of the car. It proved to be an excellent paper and he read it through carefully from the first page to the last, all the time puffing energetically at his first Thursday pipe.

A few yards from his car, the traffic flowed steadily by. From where he was sitting he could see the main entrance of Scotland Yard.

He glanced at his bullet-proof watch. 'Another minute,' he thought. 'That is, if Old Goat Beard is punctual . . .'

He was really alert now. A man was coming through the door. He was small and thin. He moved very quickly, exactly like a ferret, and he gave a friendly nod to the two guards. They were not slow in returning the salute of the Brosnian Police Chief, who had become the favourite of everybody at Scotland Yard during the three days of the International Police Conference. In his right hand he was carrying a large pigskin briefcase with a brass catch.

Everything happened according to the instructions Agaton Sax had received from the Boss. The man got into the taxi which was waiting for him and drove to St. Martin's-in-the-Fields. Agaton Sax followed.

The man got out and stood on the pavement, obviously interested in everything he saw around him. His grizzled neatly shaped goatee bobbed up and down as he watched the flocks of pigeons circling Trafalgar Square. He produced a little plastic bag, put his hand into it and took out a few dried peas, which he threw into the air.

Agaton Sax got out of his car and walked up to the man. Giving a friendly smile he raised his hat.

'Police Chief Kossoparamonescono?'

'Yes.'

'Bartolo Paragotta from the Brosnian Embassy, at your service, your Excellency. I have orders to drive your Excellency to the Brosnian Embassy, where the Ambassador is expecting you for lunch.'

For a moment Kossoparamonescono looked him straight in the eye.

'Thank you Bartolo Paragotta,' he said.

The Chief of Police got into the car, Agaton Sax saluted, closed the door behind him, and got into the driver's seat. He drove off with the chief sitting next to him.

His passenger held the briefcase pressed tightly against

his knees, as if he were afraid someone might snatch it from him. He stared straight ahead; evidently he was following the route with close attention.

'You must know London very well Mr. Paragotta,' he said after a little while.

'Yes, I do.'

'The Brosnian Embassy is in Paddington Road, isn't it?' Old Goat Beard went on, thoughtfully curling his beard round his long, thin fingers.

'Quite correct, your Excellency.'

There was a long silence. Agaton Sax drove the car up one street then down another, the Police Chief clutching his briefcase as tightly as ever. As they turned into a narrow lane called Bluff Street, the engine suddenly coughed, its regular throb was replaced by an ominous note. For a moment it spluttered and choked, then gave up and the car shuddered to a halt.

In the silence the two men faced each other.

'Has it broken down?' Old Goat Beard asked, his goatee twitching nervously.

'Yes, your Excellency, but judging from the noise, nothing more is needed than a drop of oil in the carburetter.'

'Will it take long?'

'Not at all. A matter of two or three minutes. Would your Excellency mind moving to the back seat. It's possible you might get splashed with oil when I open the bonnet.'

Old Goat Beard moved to the back. He drummed his fingers nervously on the briefcase. Now and then he glanced furtively through the car window. Whenever he did this it seemed to calm him a little.

Agaton Sax busied himself under the bonnet. He tightened a screw, the very same screw he had himself loosened an hour earlier, so that the engine would stop in Bluff Street. There was nothing wrong with the carburetter; the car had stopped because Agaton Sax wanted it to stop—and in this very street.

Three minutes later he was again at the wheel. He pulled a large box of sweets from under the seat. It was an exquisitely designed Brosnian box decorated with elephants and giraffes.

'Can I offer your Excellency a piece of genuine Brosnian chocolate?' he said with a little smile.

His passenger picked out one of the largest pieces, and munched happily.

'Thank you, Mr Paragotto,' he said, 'this chocolate always reminds me of my happy boyhood.'

'I'm glad you like it, your Excellency, otherwise I don't know how I could have managed.'

'How you could have managed, Mr Paragotta?'

'Yes, it would have been rather difficult.'

Old Goat Beard made no reply. He seemed to be pondering the meaning of these enigmatic words. Agaton Sax watched him in the rear mirror. The Police Chief yawned. His eyes seemed to be misting over. Agaton Sax gave a satisfied nod. Everything was working out well, just as he had planned. The old man leaned forward and tapped him gently on the shoulder.

'Could I have another piece of chocolate, please?'

'No, not now.'

'Oh please, Uncle, just a little bit!'

'No, chocolate is bad for your teeth, you ought to know that.'

'Oh please, *dear* Uncle, it was so delicious. Couldn't I have just one teeny-weeny little bit?'

'No. I have said no! You must listen to what Uncle tells you. No more chocolate. One piece is quite enough!'

Old Goat Beard nodded, and leant back in his seat. A smile flickered across his face; he gave a little wave, and said:

'You are a dear old Uncle, all the same.'

Agaton Sax got out of the car, and opened the rear door.

'Why are you taking away my goatee, Uncle?' Old Goat Beard asked reproachfully, as Agaton Sax gently pulled his passenger's false beard from his chin. 'You'll give it back to me tomorrow, won't you? I'm so sleepy. Good night, Uncle!'

The old Brosnian Chief of Police, who was neither old, nor Brosnian, nor Chief of Police, leant back on his seat, and fell asleep.

Agaton Sax rejoiced that the sedative he had melted into the pieces of Brosnian chocolate had taken effect. This man, who had cunningly disguised himself as Police Chief Kossoparamonescono was one of the most efficient members of the Gang who had stolen Scotland Yard's Great Code Register. The sedative Agaton Sax chose was Hypersomniumdormatolinphorpercaminalhypnosotine—a powerful, speedy but harmless drug.

The briefcase had slipped to the floor. Agaton Sax took it and turned it out quickly. Just as he thought. What he was looking for was there.

He drove at once to the nearest phone box, and rang Inspector Lispington.

'Hallo, is that Lispington speaking?'

'Who?'

'You!'

'Me?'

'Yes!'

'Yes, it's me.'

'You don't sound like you, Lispington. Is anything the matter?' Agaton Sax listened intently.

'Lispington, are you still there?'

'Where?'

'Are you there?'

'I don't know.'

'You don't know?'

'Who is it? Is that the Government?'

'No! This is Agaton Sax speaking. Don't you recognise my voice?'

He listened intently again. There was total silence.

'Hallo, Lispington, you must pull yourself together! Be a man!'

'It was a man,' Lispington moaned. 'It was him!'

'Who?'

'Old Goat Beard.'

'It was him, you said—what did he do?'

'He . . . No, you'll never believe me. I don't understand anything any more. Where are you, Agaton Sax?'

'I'm in a phone box. Please tell me what has happened!'

'I can't. I don't know. He disappeared. It *must* be him! But it's not possible! The Brosnian Chief of Police! How can such a thing happen?'

'Such a thing? What are you talking about?'

'The master stroke.'

'What master stroke?'

'Haven't you heard?'

'No.'

'The Key!'

'The Key?'

'It's gone!'

'Gone?'

'Gone!'

'Hallo! Lispington—are you there?'

'Yes, I'm here,' Lispington whispered. 'The Key has gone. The Brosnian Chief of Police has gone, too. Soon I'll be gone myself.'

'Please tell me what has happened,' Agaton Sax said firmly.

(But of course he knew very well what had happened—he just wanted Inspector Lispington's version).

'All right, I'll tell you,' Lispington said obediently. 'Shortly after half past nine this morning, Old Goat Beard arrived at Scotland Yard. To-day's session of the International Police Conference was due to start at ten o'clock. I told you Old Goat Beard was very popular with everybody in Scotland Yard. When he arrived he started chatting with two of our police sergeants who had promised yesterday to show him over Scotland Yard. They took him for a tour of the basement, and while they were down there showed him the little room where the Key to the Code Register was kept—but they did not tell him about the Key. Suddenly he drew two revolvers, one for each of the police sergeants, and forced them into the little room. Then he took the Key—it's only a little note-book, twenty-four pages in all—out of its box. After that he locked the two sergeants in the room, and ran up the stairs. In the corridor he met one of the secretaries of the Conference, and told him that he had just had an urgent message to go to the Brosnian Embassy. Then he walked out of the building, cool as a cucumber, carrying his large briefcase in his right hand. In the briefcase was the Key to the Register. It was a quarter of an hour before we found out what had happened.'

Inspector Lispington's voice broke—he could not go on.

'Hallo!' Agaton Sax shouted. 'Listen, Lispington! Listen very carefully to what I say! *I have the Key*!'

There was a sudden, heavy thud, it sounded as if someone was testing the strength of Scotland Yard's floorboards.

'Are you there, Lispington?'

'Yes, I'm here, on the floor. You are not pulling my leg, are you, Agaton Sax? Excuse me one second, will you. That's better. It's not very polite to talk to someone while you are lying on the floor. Now, Agaton Sax, I implore you—tell me the truth!'

'Of course! I have the Key, and I have Old Goat Beard as well. I knew that this would happen, but I must admit I've had some very good luck too.'

Inspector Lispington closed his eyes.

'Where are you?' he asked, almost in a whisper.

'In Bluff Street. Listen. I'll blow my whistle, that will fetch a policeman. I'll give him the receiver, and you tell him that you and I are working together. Right?'

Agaton Sax blew his whistle three times. A stalwart policeman ran up. He looked suspiciously at Agaton Sax, who gave him the receiver. The policeman took it, and listened intently.

'Yes, sir. No, sir. I understand, sir. Right, sir.'

He saluted Agaton Sax, who took the receiver again.

'Now I am leaving the false Goat Beard here in the care of this policeman,' Agaton Sax said. 'He'll bring him to you. I must go immediately. But remember this; the situation is still full of danger. We have got the Key back, but we have not found the Register. I must find it as soon as possible. There are only two men in the world who can read the Register *without* the Key. I am one of them.'

'And the other?'

'The other is *not* the Boss of the gang who has stolen the Register. If he could read it he would not have bothered to steal the Key as well. No, the other man who can read it is a man who is probably in France.'

'You know who it is then?'

'Yes. I'll tell you later.'

'And what will happen next?'

'Well, since the Boss knows that this other man in France can read the Register without the Key, what do you think he will do? He will try to contact the other man, and offer him a very substantial sum of money to read the Register.'

'Will he be willing to sell his knowledge?'

'Yes, his knowledge is no use to him unless he has the Register. He will decode it for, at a guess, a million pounds, or perhaps a little more. So, the gang's next move will be to quit this country with the Register hidden in their baggage. They will go straight to the man in France, unless . . .'

'Unless . . ?'

'Well, that is what would have happened if I had not

managed to trace the headquarters. As it is, I can stop the Boss and his gang.'

'Thank you, Agaton Sax, I'm very much obliged.'

'Don't mention it!'

'I'll be hearing from you soon, I hope?'

'Of course, see you later, Lispington.'

Agaton Sax ordered the policeman to take good care of the sleeping man without the goatee until a police car

from Scotland Yard arrived to take both the man and the briefcase to Lispington.

An hour later, Lispington was holding the briefcase in his hands. Trembling with excitement he opened it. He almost fainted, overwhelmed with joy, as he found that the Key to the Register was really there.

It is hardly necessary to point out that at the very moment Agaton Sax heard the Boss order him to contact Old Goat Beard, he realised that the Boss was planning a real master-stroke aimed at the very heart and brain of Scotland Yard.

He rubbed his hands together, well pleased with himself, and lit a pipe. Then he got into his car, put his foot on the accelerator, and shot off in the direction of the old house where, the day before, he had locked up Sycamore Flint, Belisarius Mock, Benjamin the Butler, and D.G. Twelve. They must all be in custody by now, together with the other men the Boss had sent to reinforce them. (You remember, Agaton Sax had asked Inspector Lispington to have them all arrested.) But as he sped through the streets of North-west London, Agaton Sax reflected that he might find another man at the house—a man whom the gang might be holding captive there. On the other hand it was equally possible that this man was a prisoner in the gang's headquarters in Paddington Road.

Who was this man? His identity will soon be revealed. For the time being it is sufficient to emphasise that this revelation will spotlight the methods of certain international gangs.

8

Bad news for the Boss—and Old Goat Beard again

A car was parked outside the octagonal house, 5 Bob Street. 'Scotland Yard,' Agaton Sax thought, as he walked slowly round to the back of the house. But he took nothing for granted. His profound knowledge of crime and criminals had long ago taught him to be particularly careful when approaching unfamiliar houses, even in broad daylight.

He examined the round and oval holes cut out of the hedge, and chose one of the round ones as most suitable for the shape of his body. He squeezed through, and cautiously tip-toed across the lawn. A bird chirped anxiously in a tree overhead, a cloud covered the sun—a dark and heavy thunder-cloud which cast a sinister shadow over the gaunt octagonal house and large, gloomy garden.

Agaton Sax had a sudden foreboding of some unknown looming menace. He glanced quickly round, but saw nothing to arouse his suspicion.

Two of the ground floor windows were slightly open

and he heard voices from inside the house. 'That should be the police,' he said to himself, 'but I'm not quite sure.' He crept cautiously up to the wall, flattened his body against it, and slowly edged his way towards one of the windows.

He recognised one of the voices! It was curt, metallic, deadly, imperious, and at the same time expressionless. It was, in other words, the Boss's!

Agaton Sax was stunned. Evidently the Boss had only just arrived. But what had happened? Where were the policemen Lispington had sent to collect the crooks he had locked up?

All too soon he knew the answers to these questions and a few more.

'Control from under the men Scotland are Yard?' asked the Boss in a voice that sent shivers down Agaton Sax's spine.

'Sir, indeed, sir, yes, oh! all caught them we, sir, safely and are now, sir, they, basement up in the locked, sir,' declared someone who surely must be Sycamore Flint, unless it was Belisarius Mock.

'Job have an you excellent done,' said the Boss, the ice in his voice beginning to melt a little. At the same time, he seemed to be summing up his men, as if to find out whether they would be fit to carry out the devilish schemes he was planning.

'Are who you?' he said.

'Sycamore Flint, service at, sir, always your!'

'You and?'

'Sir, D.G. Twelve.'

'You and?'

'Belisarius Mock, sir, at, sir, always service your.'

'Belisarius Mock? That's what? Mocking you me are? Me name tell real your—nick-name your not!'

'Real Belisarius Mock it but, sir, name my. One they it's the have Register, sir, in police the.'

'Ha! Ha! Register in Police the! Funny how! You and? Name your what's?'

'Sir Benjamin.'

'Sir Benjamin? Knight a baron a are or you?'

'I'm sorry, sir, I mean, Sir, Benjamin. Name my Benjamin, sir, is. Called I also am P. Thirteen.'

'Enough that's.'

Agaton Sax nodded to himself. The Boss's system was exactly what he had expected. The Boss very seldom showed himself to the members of the gang. Diabolically shrewd, he kept his identity hidden from all his confederates. As a rule, all his criminal operations were carried out according to secret orders he sent out himself, first to a number of deputy directors, from them to junior sub-directors, and finally to the ordinary members of the gang. As he crouched under the window, Agaton Sax was sure, although he couldn't see him, that the Boss would be wearing a black mask.

Agaton Sax got the impression that the Boss was walking up and down the room. He heard him go on:

'I'll speak in plain English now. Listen very carefully all of you. We have struck Scotland Yard a terrific blow—probably the greatest blow in the annals of crime. What exactly we have done I can't tell you, because that is still top secret. But you can take my word for it: *Scotland Yard is paralysed*! At this very moment the enemy is reeling. Two days ago I sent him to his knees with a punch on the head. Now I've knocked him out and he's done for. Remember this! You are witnessing the most dazzling success ever achieved in the glorious history of crime. Some day, far, far off in the distant future, you will be able to tell your children, and your grand-children, and your great-grand-children, tell them with pride, "Daddy was there!" or "Grandfather was there!" or "Great Grandfather was there!" That's all I want to say. Remember we shall meet at 13B Paddington Road shortly. All deputy directors, junior sub-directors, and assistants have been ordered to be there at twenty-three hours. I warn all of you not to . . .'

The Boss never finished his sentence. His dark eyes glowed menacingly through the holes in his mask.

'Was what that?' his voice cut the silence like a whip lash.

'Mean you what do, sir?'

'Hear you didn't?'

Indeed, they all heard. From the street the sound of a car was heard approaching the octagonal house. The Boss rushed to the half-open window. Swift as lightning, Agaton Sax drew back, and melted into the shadow of a large branch. He held his breath. Once again, a pregnant silence descended upon the room where the rogues were waiting, their hearts pounding with fear.

From the street came a squeal of brakes, then the car stopped dead. A man flung himself out, and dashed across the lawn with such a turn of speed that even Agaton Sax had some difficulty in catching a glimpse of his face.

Inside the house the rogues drew their revolvers as one man.

The Boss stood motionless in the middle of the room, glaring at the door with such ferocity that it seemed his gaze must pierce the thick oak panels which the stranger was battering with flailing fists, while at the same time, babbling incoherently.

'The quick open door—in me let—open in me quick door the let—door the in quick let open me—let me open quick in the door!'

Suddenly the door burst open, apparently of its own accord, and the stranger shot forward into the Boss's arms. At this he got such a shock that he almost collapsed, but even in his confused state of mind he did manage to remember that he had a message to deliver, and once again through quivering lips came a torrent of words:

'Spectacles chap with the sitting was who car the in from snatched beard the goat the goat the beard with man him handed and copper to over a, sir! Old and man that the with beard goat without goat or beard was . . .'

'Shut up, you ignorant, incompetent lout—you don't even know the basic principles of your scramble-talk grammar! How dare you come stumbling in here with your miserable, rambling, delirious poppycock. Say what you are trying to say in plain English!'

The Boss, speechless with rage, shook his fist at the poor unhappy newcomer, who nodded rapidly, then swallowed nervously, and repeated what he had just said. His scramble-talk was grammatically quite correct. The truth was that the Boss, for all his intelligence and shrewdness, had been incapable of grasping the significance of his underling's words. Agaton Sax on the other hand, had got the gist at once in spite of the scramble.

'Sir, you thank—thank you, sir, I mean,' the stranger said. 'I was just trying to tell you, sir, that the chap with the spectacles who was sitting in the car snatched the goatee from the man with the goatee, and handed him over to a copper, sir! And the old man with or without the goatee was . . .'

The Boss, hearing these words, was struck dumb for a moment, but making a gigantic effort to steady himself, took a deep breath and said, coldly:

'Up shut! Repeat don't that! *Where is the pigskin portfolio?*'

'The skinpig p . . . the pinskig portfolio, sir—I—he—the chap with the spectacles took it, sir!'

'He took it? Just like that?'

'Yes, sir, when he had snatched the goatee from the man with the goatee, he went to a phone box, and he took the portfolio with him, and the copper took the chap with the goatee—I mean the man who didn't have one.'

'Where is S.F. Seventeen?' the Boss roared.

By this time the poor man was shaking convulsively, and his knees were knocking together so violently with fright, that he collapsed on the floor.

'Did you say S.F. Seventeen, sir?'

'I did! Meaning the man with the spectacles, as you call him. The man who took the goatee and the portfolio! *Where is he?*'

'Know I that don't, no, sir, but he took the car too, and beat it.'

'And beat it?! So you just let him go—you allowed him to vanish into thin air—you intolerable, senseless, useless good-for-nothing!' shouted the Boss, who had again flown into a towering passion.

'I couldn't stop him, sir, I really couldn't, there wasn't time. He was so quick, sir. I followed him all the time, just as I had been ordered, sir, to make sure that everything was O.K., sir, so that nobody could come and take him by surprise, sort of protecting him, sir, just as you told me. But what can you do, sir, when . . . well, sir, I don't know, sir, it all happened so quickly, sir, and he was . . .'

The Boss stared at him, gimlet eyed, and every man in the room quivered like an aspen leaf. He spoke again, but this time his cold fury was aimed at them all:

'Which of you is the real S.F. Seventeen?'

'Me, sir,' Sycamore Flint quavered.

'And you did not come to 13B Paddington Road last night?'

'No, sir, I swear I didn't, sir!'

'And I did not speak to you and order you to meet the man with the false beard this morning?'

'No, sir, as you say, sir, I swear you didn't!'

'And why didn't I speak to you last night?'

'Because I was a prisoner here, sir, I swear!'

The Boss beat his fists against his forehead, and tore his hair in an outburst of impotent fury.

'Agaton Sax!' he cried, his voice choked with emotion. (When he heard that, Agaton Sax was tempted to answer 'Yes, what is it, I'm here!')

'Agaton Sax,' he repeated. 'I should have known! He tricked me into believing that he was S.F. Seventeen! It was he I sent out to meet our agent with the false goatee who had stolen the Key to the Register! It was he, Agaton Sax, who stole the Key and the goatee—he—the scoundrel—the traitor—O false and treacherous Agaton Sax! What a fool I have been! But remember—I'm still the Boss! I'll get him in the end! I'll win a glorious victory over that fat little man with his ridiculous moustache and his priggish air. We must be off! Follow me. We'll go straight to Headquarters. No, wait a minute, we mustn't forget those fellows from Scotland Yard! Go and fetch them from the basement.'

Agaton Sax needed just three seconds to decide exactly what to do.

The man he wanted to set free—whose identity will soon be revealed—could definitely not be locked up in this house, for if he had been, the Boss would have ordered his men to take him along to Headquarters with the policemen. The only conclusion Agaton Sax could draw from all he had heard was that the man he was interested in was held captive at 13B Paddington Road.

As quick as lightning, or even quicker, Agaton Sax slipped away through the same hole in the hedge he had used to come in, and made a dash for his car. Breaking all sorts of traffic laws and speed regulations he careered half across London, pursued from time to time by policemen on motor-cycles, who blew their whistles and shook their fists as he politely raised his hat, then slipped off before they could stop him.

'I have a four minute start on the Boss and his men,' he thought as he parked in a narrow street near the gang's headquarters, and ran to 13B.

He banged on the front door.

'What station?'

'Next stop, Braxington.'

The door creaked on its hinges as it was opened a fraction.

'Orders from the Boss, give me the key to the basement,' Agaton Sax said, making his voice sound as villainous as possible.

'Are who you? Your what's number?'

'Q Fourteen.'

'In come,' said the man, who was wearing dark glasses. 'Key the here is. Know you do way the?'

'No.'

'On straight, stairs the down, left turn.'

'Good very, you thank.'

Agaton Sax unlocked the door to the basement with the key he had been given and ran down the stairs two at a time. The whole operation was at stake! Success depended entirely upon his speed and resolution. Nothing could stop him now. At the foot of the stairs he came to a dark corridor. Feeling his way with his right hand, he soon found a door. Slowly and cautiously he turned the handle. Not surprisingly the door was locked. He knocked softly and said in a whisper:

'Takamossopontarastanklene Kossoparamonesconoh'ministropolissoro, eh?' Which is Brosnian, and means literally, 'Are you Police Chief Kossoparamonescono?'

'Tompokorontossarimanatele podaministratossoroman Brosnikatatelementele polis he?'

('Don't ask stupid questions! Of course I am the Brosnian Police Chief.')

Sax—talarmissontorkoro h'*Agaton*, korintissimo.'

('I am Agaton Sax, and I will open the door for you.')

'Prodonessarantarakatameno Agaton agate Sax Mr.'

('That is very kind of you, Mr Agaton Sax.')

Agaton Sax unlocked the door with his transistor-powered skeleton key. Before him stood the genuine Old Goat Beard—the authentic Brosnian Police Chief, the one and only Kossoparamonescono. In the dim light shed by the only lamp in his small cell, the minister scrutinised his liberator, so as to make sure that this fat little man really was Agaton Sax, of whose wonderful exploits he

had heard so often. After a moment's hesitation, his face cleared, he flung wide his arms, clasped Agaton Sax to his breast, and, kissing him on both cheeks, exclaimed joyfully:

'H'agate Agaton herokossomostratos p'Sax!'

('How happy I am! You are indeed Agaton Sax.')

'Shsh!' said Agaton Sax, speaking English. 'Remember, we are still in the lion's den. At any minute the whole gang will be here to plan their next move. I'll explain everything to you later. Please wait here while I scout round to see if there's a back door we can escape through. I won't be a minute.'

He soon found a narrow door which he could open easily with his skeleton key. Then he hurried upstairs to the guard at the door, and said :

'Everything is O.K. in the basement. I have orders to keep watch there. I'll report to you again at two o'clock.'

'K.O.' grunted the guard, chewing on an extinguished cigar.

Agaton Sax sped back to the authentic Brosnian Police Chief.

'Come, my dear friend,' he whispered, taking Old Goat Beard by the arm and gently propelling him along the dark corridor. 'They are just arriving, can you hear them?'

The Brosnian Police Chief nodded. His chin and his elegant, neatly trimmed goatee were set as he thought of the rogues who had knidnapped him so insolently on his arrival in London two days earlier.

9

An advertisement in *The Times*

Agaton Sax was right, two cars had drawn up. The gang hustled themselves out and pushed through the front door. They were led by the Boss, still wearing his black mask. His words lashed the air as he gave a few curt commands, before hurrying off to the secret radio room from which he issued all his orders.

In the large hall, the rogues listened for the words they knew would soon come out of the loud-speaker behind the cactus. They were glancing uneasily about them, and every now and then two whispered words could be heard. Those words were : *Agaton Sax*.

Suddenly the metallic voice clanged from the loud-speaker :

'Attention everybody ! A traitor is in our midst. You are all familiar with his hateful name—Agaton Sax. He is our mortal enemy. He is worse than Scotland Yard, worse than the International Police Force. It's out of the question for us to tolerate his prowling the streets of London any longer, so we must put him out of the way. When we've got him safely locked up, we'll demand a ransom of £14,000,000. No one's likely to fork out that much for him, so he won't bother us any more. But before we catch him, we must make a laughing-stock of him. This will be the criminal master-stroke of the century. My plans are already made, and the whole gang will get their orders within minutes. Those of you here now must proceed as follows: Go to *The Three-Masted Schooner* in Brighton at 14.00 hours to-day. The address is 3 Short-cut Road. When you get there, await further orders from me. But before you set off, you must all buy certain articles of clothing and other things which you'll find on a list I have drawn up for you.'

'But about the what money, sir?' one of the men said. 'Am broke I.'

'So broke are you, you are?' the Boss answered icily. 'I am not in the least interested in your private financial affairs, is that understood? And don't interrupt me! You all know where to find my deputy director, D.A. Thirteen. He will give you £17 each—in good currency. You are strictly forbidden to use counterfeit money—not even a counterfeit penny. When you have got your £17, proceed independently to Brighton. On no account must you go there together! And remember, *nobody knows anybody else*. Now for your disguise. You will all be dressed as early nineteenth century sailors. Remember that—you are all sailors. Walk like sailors, speak like sailors. Is that clear? Do you all know what a sailor looks like? Good. You must all carry Sailors' Certificates, these Certificates are already forged for you, with false names in them. Is everything clear? Now go to my deputy director, D.A. Thirteen, and get your money and your certificates. He'll need your signatures for them.'

'What is a sir-fisticuffs, please, sir?' one of the rogues enquired.

'A Sailor's Certificate, you numskull, is a sailor's passport. Every sailor must carry one or he can't be a sailor. Is that clear?'

'Yes, oh, thank, sir, you.'

'Are you all quite clear what you have to do?'

'Yes, sir. We'll set sail, sir, so to speak,' several of the men answered.

'Good! Carry out my orders!'

Completely flabbergasted by what he had heard, Old Goat Beard looked at Agaton Sax, who nodded thoughtfully.

'Will you help me to catch this gang?' he whispered.

'Tarakosoopomantrantara h', agate Agaton troddandronda Sax Mr.'

('Indeed, I would love to help you, Mr Agaton Sax.')

'Good. Follow me.'

'Travalleramontorossono Scot—terramontrosantanaraland frato-lustrana Yard-h'.'

('Come, let us speed to Scotland Yard.')

'No, no, Mr Kossoparamonescono, that would be much too dangerous. It is too early to trap the gang yet. We must let them operate unsuspectingly for another twenty-four hours. Then we'll strike, and our success will be even more dazzling than you expect. Trust me. Let's go!'

They quickly went out through the narrow door Agaton Sax had opened on his brief earlier reconaissance.

'Listen carefully,' he said, as they reached the pavement. 'We'll each concentrate on one rogue—you take the one who resembles you, and I'll take the one who looks like me. You follow your man and I'll follow mine. Don't lose sight of him. Shadow him as he enters the shop to buy his sailor's rig. Shadow him as he comes out again. Then have him arrested; hand him over to Scotland Yard, but don't tell the detectives what you are going to do next. Tell Scotland Yard that you have instructions from me to disguise yourself as a sailor. Last, but not least, shave off your beard.'

'Gotobarbarossara shavatacaoffata, h'!' the Police Chief exclaimed, furious at the very thought.

('Shave off my beard? Never!')

'But you must realise that none of the rogues is wearing a beard, so you can't either, since you will have to be disguised as one of them.'

'Of course none of them has a beard like mine! Just let them try!'

'But they would recognise you! Please! You must look exactly like the man you have arrested!'

With a bitter little gesture Old Goat Beard agreed to this disagreeable proposition. Police Chief he might be, but he could not refuse to obey an order coming from Agaton Sax.

'As soon as you have shaved off your beard,' Agaton Sax went on, 'you must go to Brighton. I'll meet you at the station.'

'And after that?'

'A very natural question. Something really interesting, I promise.'

Briefly Agaton Sax told the Police Chief what would happen during the next four or five hours. Old Goat Beard listened keenly.

'You haven't changed your mind about taking part in this expedition?' Agaton Sax asked.

'I? Changed my mind? Never! I want to crush those scoundrels who attacked me and locked me up!'

Keeping a watchful eye on the street, which was still empty, Agaton Sax went on:

'You have not yet told me how it all happened. How did they manage to kidnap you?'

'I arrived at London Airport the night before the opening of the International Police Conference. There were two detectives—or rather, that's what they called themselves—to meet me. I followed them, quite unsuspecting. As a matter of fact, they were two monstrous, outrageous rogues, who suddenly overpowered me, robbed me of my passport and all my other papers, and locked me up in the basement cell from which you have just rescued me.'

'And the Boss sent another man to the Police Conference in your place,' Agaton Sax added grimly.

'Another man, what do you mean, Mr Sax?'

The Police Chief turned sharply, surprise and indignation on his face.

'They dressed up a man of exactly your size, and gave him a beard, cut exactly like yours. This man spoke Brosnian fluently. He presented himself at Scotland Yard as the Brosnian Police Chief, Kossoparamonescono. As he had your passport and nobody in Scotland Yard knew you personally, everybody was convinced that he was you.'

The Police Chief gasped.

'This is outrageous! What a vile and corrupt villain! And . . . and then?'

'Then the false Brosnian Police Chief became the favourite of everybody in Scotland Yard and at the Conference. He was commonly called Old Goat Beard—a nick-name which seemed to delight him.'

'Old Goat Beard? I never heard anything so insolent in all my life! And then?'

'Then he managed to steal Scotland Yard's top secret Code Register. But don't worry, I have already caught him!'

'You have caught him. By Jove, I wish I had him here!'

'Hush! They are coming! Now you choose your man, and remember, he must be the same size as you. Don't lose sight of him!'

The rogues were streaming out of No. 13B Paddington Road. Agaton Sax and Kossoparamonescono watched them closely, and within seconds selected one each to shadow. A nod signalled that all was well and they separated. Keeping some twenty yards behind, Agaton Sax discreetly followed the corpulent little fellow he had chosen, shadowing him to the nearest bus-stop. The man jumped on a bus, with Agaton Sax on his heels. He got off at Associated Drapers, the well-known store, where he took the lift up to the Fancy-dress Department on the fourth floor. Then he took the slip of paper which the Boss had given him out of his pocket. It was obviously a list of the things he needed for his disguise. He chose several garments, and tried them on in front of one of the large mirrors.

Agaton Sax approached the counter and stood by the man. He also brought a slip of paper out of his pocket. The little rogue stared at him.

'B Twelve am I, Braxington stop next,' Agaton Sax whispered. 'Clothes buy my too I'll.'

'Am C Four I,' the man mumbled. 'But don't understand I.' Must have really we scramble *clothes*, too? All what about this is?'

'Decision the Boss's it's,' Agaton Sax murmured. 'Get when outside we a taxi take I'll. Share with you will me it? Pay I'll it for. You coming are?'

'Of course—no, course of, mean I.'

They waited for the clothes they had chosen to be wrapped up, paid for them, and went out into the street, where the traffic was flowing past in a broad, roaring river of cars and buses. Agaton Sax hailed a taxi.

'Can you take us to Brighton? We want No. 3 Short-Cut Road!' Agaton Sax asked the driver.

'Just a minute,' the fat little rogue said suddenly.

'What is it?'

'I left my wallet on the counter! I won't be a second.' So saying he jumped out of the taxi and dashed off into the crowd. In a flash Agaton Sax realised that the man was lying, using this simple ruse to make good his escape. With the speed of a greyhound Agaton Sax was after his man, who, poor wretch, suddenly saw a policeman not fifteen yards ahead! In such a desperate situation, he had no choice: he dodged back into the store and shot through the crowd like a torpedo. He plunged headlong into an empty lift, pressed the button, and reached the top floor at the very same instant as Agaton Sax got to the lift gates below.

Without stopping to think Agaton Sax began to run up the stairs, but before he was half way up he realised that the lift was coming down again with the man inside. A second later it was going up again. By the time this manœuvre had been repeated five times, Agaton Sax was very near to losing his temper, something which only happened about twice a year. With a great effort he controlled his rage, stretched out his hand, threw a switch, and cut off the electric current. Every light in the store went out, and the lift stopped half way between the second and third floors.

At this point the Manager himself appeared, carrying a magnificent electric torch in his right hand. He made his way through the dense crowd of excited, rather confused customers. When he saw Agaton Sax standing by the switch, he blew his whistle—it was made of pure gold—to summon all the store detectives. They came at once, converging on Agaton Sax from every corner of the shop.

'Arrest this man!' the Manager said, pointing to Agaton Sax.

'Just a minute, sir,' said Agaton Sax, with great dignity, raising his right hand. 'Will you be good enough to read this letter?'

He handed a paper to the Manager, who, on reading it, turned first pale, then red, then pale again. The letter ran as follows:

TO WHOM IT MAY CONCERN.

The bearer of this letter is Agaton Sax. In all vicissitudes, he represents not only himself, but also Scotland Yard and the International Police Force. Whoever he apprehends, arrests, or takes into custody, should consider himself veritably apprehended, arrested, or taken into custody. (Even if it is you yourself.) Never oppose him. He is invincible.

Lispington,
Scotland Yard.

The Manager's bow was low. 'At your service, Mr Agaton Sax, sir,' he said. 'Who, in this establishment would you like to apprehend, arrest, or take into custody?'

He made a sweeping gesture, inviting Agaton Sax to indicate any customers or detectives he might wish to arrest. But Agaton Sax pointed to the door of the lift-shaft.

'The man in the lift,' he said. 'And I want his parcel, too, please.'

C Four was brought down to the ground floor and arrested immediately by four policemen. Agaton Sax said goodbye to the Manager; the customers went back to their shopping, and the life of the store returned to normal.

But for Agaton Sax there was no time to lose. He bought a day old copy of *The Times*, and eagerly scanned the advertisement pages. Very soon he found what he was looking for. Triumphantly he took a red-and-blue pencil from his pocket and marked an advertisement that read as follows:

IF YOU ARE A REAL OLD SALT—READ THIS! Would you like to sail on the Seven Seas? Do you have a heart that beats faster when the tang of salt is in your nostrils? Are you dreaming of foreign countries and far-away beaches? Would you like to plough through Atlantic rollers on board my three-masted barque *Esmeralda*? If you really are an Old Salt, and if you are badly in need of cash—come along and join my crew. Embark on the greatest Adventure of your life! All I ask is that you wear the clothes of a Jack Tar in Nelson's day. I need 40 men now. Apply tomorrow, 14.00 hours sharp, to *The Three-Masted Schooner*, 3 Short-Cut Road, Brighton. Bring your seaman's passport. The *Esmeralda* weighs anchor tomorrow, 18.00 hours.

Archibald Duck,
Multi-millionaire.

Agaton Sax nodded his head thoughtfully. When he had heard the Boss order his men to buy fancy-dress costumes and go to Brighton he had known at once that this was yet another diabolical scheme. He had been sure then that the Boss was acting on something he had just seen in a newspaper. Now his suspicions were confirmed. He knew exactly what the Boss's plans were, and he knew too, how the Boss could be stopped. For some time now Agaton Sax had known only too well that the Boss was the most super-intelligent gang leader he had ever had to deal with. This time he was heading for real danger.

He had to get back to his hotel at once. He called a taxi, and on the journey jotted down one or two important ideas in his secret note-book. When he arrived at the hotel the hall porter met him. He had a telegram in his hand which he gave to Agaton Sax, saying, 'This has just arrived, sir.'

10

Archibald Duck—millionaire

As he tore open the telegram Agaton Sax had a sudden premonition of danger. Then he read:

> Dear Colleague, I am so sorry, but I cannot accompany you. The Brosnian Ambassador wants me immediately. I will say nothing to Lispington. Good luck!
>
> Kossoparamonescono.

'This won't upset my plans at all,' Agaton Sax muttered thoughtfully, putting on a false moustache. 'I can manage the Boss alone. Perhaps Archibald Duck, the multi-millionaire, will be of some help too.'

He changed his clothes quickly, putting on the red, white and blue sailor's rig he had bought, and smartening it up with a few gleaming medals from C Four's parcel. Then he picked up the telephone and asked for Scotland Yard.

'Is that you, Lispington?'

'That depends. Who is asking?'

'Agaton Sax—I swear. Listen, Lispington. The situation is still perilous. Old Goat Beard will ring you in a few minutes.'

'What's that you say? Old Goat Beard calling me? But that's impossible! He's in custody. For Heaven's sake—Great Scott! What did you say? No—this is too horrible.'

'Take it easy, Lispington! I mean the real, the genuine Old Goat Beard.'

'The real, the genuine? By Jove, Agaton Sax, you're terrifying me! Are there two Old Goat Beards?'

Briefly Agaton Sax put his colleague in the picture. Lispington groaned.

'But I have just informed the British Government that the Brosnian Police Chief has proved to be a totally unscrupulous crook and swindler!'

'Have you, that's bad,' Agaton Sax said, frowning. 'Then you must inform the British Government immediately that he is *not* a crook and a swindler—otherwise both the British and the Brosnian Governments will be extremely cross with you. Hallo! Hallo! Are you still there, Lispington? Why do you sound so far away? Ah, now I can hear you better. Listen carefully. As I have just told you, the danger is by no means past.'

'But we have got the Key back, haven't we? They can't read the Key without the Code—no, I mean, they can't read the Code without the Key, can they?'

'That's true. They can't. But there are two people who can, as I have already told you.'

'What two people?'

'Myself—and another man.'

'Who are you? No, I'm sorry, I mean—who's the other man?'

'That I don't know yet. But the Boss knows, and he is on his way to meet him.'

'We must stop him!' Lispington's voice was almost a scream.

'Exactly. That's what I'm about to do. Within three days, at the most, I'll hand him over to you, Lispington.'

'Can't we help you?'

'No, I'm sorry, that would be too risky. You'll hear from me again. Any if haven't had you news by me from Saturday, must enquiries about make me you Atlantic on the,' he added mysteriously.

'Hallo! Agaton Sax—what was that—was that you? I don't understand a word! You must not speak Brosnian until I have learnt it.'

'That was only scramble-talk, my dear Lispington,' Agaton Sax said kindly. 'See you later.'

He hung up. As he walked down to his car, he remembered that he had heard several things about Archibald

Duck, the multi-millionaire. He was a very rich man who had never had to work for his living. (Though it was rumoured that he had put up several sets of bookshelves in his early twenties.) He had wonderful ideas, which he realised with exceptional energy. Three years ago he had turned his estate into an amusement park, so that he could amuse himself without being disturbed by other people. Now he had apparently turned his attention to ships and shipping. He knew absolutely nothing about the sea, but having read in a newspaper that the old three-masted barque *Esmeralda* (built in 1805) was for sale, had decided to buy it. The cost was a mere £74,000, cash on delivery. Then he had advertised for a crew in *The Times*. This advertisement must have been spotted by the Boss, who, with his quick intelligence and powerful imagination, had realised that this was a wonderful opportunity to get out of England without being observed by Scotland Yard or itinerant peripatetic representatives of the International Police Force.

Agaton Sax drove into Brighton shortly before 14.00 hours. He found 3 Short-Cut Road without any difficulty. Behind a thick hedge was a magnificent manor house in an equally magnificent park. In the park was a wonderful merry-go-round, and an impressive switchback.

A tall, lean man was standing on the steps of the manor, waiting for his guests. He looked about fifty and was dressed in the uniform of a sea-captain at the time of Trafalgar. Under his right arm was a long telescope, in his left hand he held up a rolled-up chart. He put the telescope to his eye as he saw Agaton Sax's car approaching. Focusing carefully on the little man in the car, he nodded with pleasure and murmured:

'Very good, indeed! He looks like an excellent sailor.'

Then, with a sudden twist, he trained his telescope on a new object, and two red spots of excitement showed on his cheeks.

'By Jove!' he exclaimed, 'there are dozens of 'em!' Eagerly pressing the telescope still closer to his eye, he added, 'This is wonderful—couldn't be better—there must be at least thirty-five.'

What he had seen was not one car—it was a crowd of cars, or an armada of cars, as he would prefer to call it—and they were approaching from all directions, surging up the drive to the magnificent manor house, where they drew up with a squeal of brakes. It seemed that every door opened at the same moment, and out of the cars tumbled a whole fleet of sailors, dressed in red, white and blue jerseys. Brightly coloured handkerchiefs were tied round their necks and they wore pirate knives in their belts. All of them carried telescopes, blunderbusses, pistols, compasses, hammocks, boat hooks, small anchors, hawsers, grapnels, tarpaulins, sea boots. Nothing was missing. They all walked with the slightly rocking gait so characteristic of the real Old Salt in the good old days.

'Excellent, excellent, indeed,' Archibald Duck muttered as he watched the motley crew approach the manor house, waddling like a procession of dressed-up ducks.

Agaton Sax, too, had waddled out of his car and joined the others. He looked exactly like C Four—who was now in safe hands at Scotland Yard—and not one of the rogues could possibly have suspected that his greatest mortal enemy was closely watching his every move and constantly listening to all that was said. Agaton Sax took a particular interest in twenty-eight of the imposters who were carrying between them fourteen boxes. It was clear from the care they took that the contents were priceless. Agaton Sax had no doubt that the twenty-eight false sailors were carrying off Scotland Yard's great Secret Code Register of Current Criminals.

Now Archibald Duck knew absolutely nothing of the superbly ingenious plan worked out by the Boss. He snapped his telescope shut, raised his right arm like a Field-Marshal, or perhaps an Admiral of the Fleet, and called out:

'Welcome, Old Salts. Come in and sign on. I'll pay you better than any other captain in the Northern Hemisphere.'

They flocked into the large hall, where Archibald Duck's two butlers were seated at large tables covered with thick bundles of pound notes.

'Please, gentlemen, form a queue. Have your seamen's passports ready—sign on—and draw your first pay in advance.'

Who could resist such an invitation? Certainly not the rogues, who rushed the tables, waving their false passports. The butlers carefully examined the documents handed over to them by the rogues. (The butlers, by the way, knew absolutely nothing about the sea, nor had they ever heard of seamen's passports.)

'Excellent,' said one of the butlers.

'This is extraordinary,' said the other.

'I never saw such wonderful service records before.'

'Nor did I. This man must be the best sailor in the Northern Hemisphere.'

'But this one is even better, look.'

'This man has sailed on fifty-five ships—he must be a real expert.'

'Fine, fine,' said Archibald Duck, beaming happily. 'I'll have a crew of really first class sailors.' Raising his voice, he continued: 'Listen, all of you. Is there a captain among you? And a mate?'

'Aye, aye, sir,' three of the rogues answered.

'I'm a captain, sir.'

'You have a captain's ticket?'

'Of course I have.'

'Good. Excellent. Are there any mates here?'

'Yes, sir, I'm a first mate.'

'And I'm a second rate, sir.'

There was an ominous silence. Then a harsh whisper 'You blockhead!'

The same harsh voice—which belonged, of course, to the Boss—spoke out:

'He's sorry, sir, he means that he's a second mate, sir.'

'Splendid! Is there a third mate here, too?'

There was another silence, this time not so ominous. Then, again, the Boss's harsh voice rang out:

'C Four!'

Agaton Sax reacted swiftly.

'I'm a third mate,' he called out in C Four's voice.

Agaton Sax was most anxious to find out who the Boss was, but he dared not look round. 'I'll find him all right,' he thought, tightening the belt round his waist in a gesture of resolution and decision. Archibald Duck spoke again:

'Gentlemen, let us all go on board and make ready to sail. Our Great Adventure lies ahead. America is waiting on the other side of the Atlantic.'

'Hip, hip, hurrah!' The rogues responded with three echoing cheers. As they rolled cheerfully down the steps of the manor, out into the drive, and down to the harbour, they were watched by a hundred or so slightly surprised Brightonians, of whom some seventy at least conjectured about the contents of the fourteen boxes, and wondered why a company of touring comedians should be handling them with such care.

In the bay, *Esmeralda* lay at anchor. She was, indeed, beautiful to behold. There was solid strength as well as elegant grace in her lines. Anyone seeing her, however inexperienced as a seaman, could not help being impressed by her tall masts, the intricacy of her brand new rigging, and the glorious set of her sails.

Of the thirty-five rogues present only three had any sea-going experience at all. They were the men who had volunteered as captain, first mate, and second mate. Agaton Sax was a skilled yachtsman, and he relied on this. The captain, or P Fourteen, took command with determination and grim energy. He was a big, hefty man with carroty hair, and a beard (false) of the same colour. He divided up his crew into two groups, and marched them on board two launches moored at the quayside. Three of the sailors immediately fell into the water and had to be fished out by their mates. Four others got seasick before the launches had cast off. Two others protested strongly against the idea of sailing to America in anything so small. All the time, Archibald Duck stood motionless in the stern of one of the launches, his clean-cut features turned towards *Esmeralda*.

There were moments of utter confusion; but at last, with a tremendous effort, all the oarsmen managed to pull together and in the same direction. Twenty minutes later they had covered the whole distance—one hundred and ten yards—to the *Esmeralda*. Everyone managed to get on board; then there was confusion for another twenty minutes before the captain took possession of the bridge.

'All hands on deck!' he commanded.

'Where is the deck?' a worried voice enquired.

'You must say: "Where is the deck, *sir*!"' the captain shouted furiously.

'Where is the deck, sir?'

'Right! From now on I am *sir*, because I am the *captain*. Is that understood? As for you—you who ask me where the deck is—you ignorant landlubber—didn't they teach you anything at school? You'll never get on in life if you don't know how to address your captain.'

P Fourteen tore at his hair in despair. Then desperately set about explaining how to set sails; make fast ropes; weigh anchor and then set the hawse-blocks. He shouted furiously at his crew, enraged by the blank look on their faces, till he suddenly realised that so little did they know of nautical terms, they thought he was speaking in Scramble-talk. Once that misunderstanding had been cleared up, most of the men went to work with gusto.

But the danger was by no means past. The captain and the three mates had their work cut out. Not only were there orders to give, but every few minutes they had to climb the shrouds, the yards and the topsail tyes in order to rescue men who were stuck, or hopelessly lost, in the rigging. They had to avert every imaginable kind of disaster. Down on the deck, three or four men were wandering about, demanding loudly whether anyone had seen the main mast, if someone could tell them the difference between port and starboard, or why there were no funnels.

Not without reason Agaton Sax had misgivings as to the outcome of this strange expedition. One good thing was that fine weather had been forecast for the next few days. Another was that he himself had spent a whole year before the mast in his youth. He was quite at home with snap hooks, thimbles, davits, signal halyards, slippery hitches, jacks, tacks, crawfeet, dead eyes, and so forth and knew how to give orders for carrying out any manœuvre. A sudden puff of wind filled the sails, and *Esmeralda* was under way, slipping gracefully through the water.

'He's moving! He's sailing!' shouted several men together.

'Fools! Idiots! This is a *she*, not a *he*!' the captain roared from the bridge. 'Don't think I'm criticising you, you lazy good-for-nothings, but how do you expect me to sail this ship with a pack of half-witted sleep-walkers for a crew? By thunder, I'll send the lot of you back to school as soon as we get to America!'

But nobody heard what he said, for the whole crew threw their caps in the air and cheered at the tops of their voices.

'Hip, hip, hurrah! Hip, hip, hurrah! We're sailing!'

Archibald Duck, the multi-millionaire, had climbed to the top of the main mast, where he stood motionless, the telescope glued to his right eye. He was triumphant; his cheeks glowed, his heart was filled with joy and pride. At last he was on the open sea. At last his beautiful ship, *Esmeralda*, was challenging the Atlantic, sailed by an exceptionally competent crew. At last he was on his way to America.

Or, to be more correct, that's what Archibald Duck thought.

11

A well-planned shortage of soup

As the Harbour Master and the officials of the Harbour Board were that very afternoon preparing for Brighton's annual regatta, it happened that no competent representative of the Authorities noticed the extraordinary manœuvres and eccentric zigzag course of the three-masted barque *Esmeralda* across the Harbour mouth.

The only official who, with growing amazement, watched this astonishing spectacle, was Mr Bluewater, a retired town clerk from Nottinghamshire. As he sat on his veranda, he tried to calculate how many thousand pounds it would cost to repair the vessel after she had run aground a mile or two east of the harbour.

But of course Mr. Bluewater did not know Agaton Sax was on board. Thanks to his skill and experience, the *Esmeralda* cleared the shoals. For an instant, the great sails hung loose, she wallowed uncertainly in the waves, then she went about, and the fine old words of command came across on the wind:

'Ready about!'

'Lee-o!'

'Duck heads!'

'Square the yards!'

No wonder that *Esmeralda* made headway in such competent hands. The spray flew off her bows, the wind sang in her rigging, her canvas was at full stretch—and seven men were sick over the port rail.

Agaton Sax climbed the shrouds. His watchful eye surveyed the deck. Where was the Boss? Who was he?

Agaton recognised a few of the men, but they were just ordinary criminals; others he knew could not possibly be the Boss; they were too tall or too stout, or too stupid.

Suddenly he pricked up his ears. There was that voice again, taut, cold and peremptory. It was impossible to say where it came from. The Boss and one or two of his most trusted confederates must have secretly installed a microphone and loudspeaker on board. The voice could be heard all over the ship:

'Hands all the except helmsman behind assemble after-cabin the, will served where supper fifteen at 20.00 hours be!'

Archibald Duck, who was still scanning the horizon through his telescope, heard the Boss's strange order, frowned and called out:

'Did I hear someone talking backwards? That is strictly forbidden on board the *Esmeralda*! The Merchant Shipping Acts are very strict on this point.'

The captain took a large bite from his twist of tobacco, threw back his flaming red head, and called to the owner of the *Esmeralda*:

'No, sir, no-one wasn't talking backwards. That was just nautical talk, sir. An order.'

'An order?' said Archibald Duck surprised. 'And what did it mean?'

'It meant, sir, that we must lower away the peak and throat halyards, bringing down the gaff-topsail, if you see what I mean, sir. And that order must be carried out at 20.15 to-night, sir.'

'I see,' said Archibald Duck, his face brightening. 'How fascinating these sea terms are—and how useful.'

Agaton Sax climbed down. He had spotted the loud speaker he had been looking for. It was installed behind a coil of rope. If he followed the thin cable connecting the loudspeaker with the microphone, he would discover the room from which the Boss was directing operations.

Very carefully the ace-detective made his way to the stern of the vessel, following the cable. He nodded to himself. This was exactly what he had suspected: the cable led to the galley.

He peered through the galley window, and saw a very small man standing at the stove. He was stirring an immense stock-pot which must have held at least ten gallons of some sort of ship's soup.

'That's very odd,' Agaton Sax thought. He went into the galley and looked carefully round. There was no sign of a microphone.

'Lots here I've thick of soup ship's—like you would to a have drop?' the little fellow asked, flourishing the ladle.

'Thanks, no,' Agaton Sax said, going quickly outside. 'Very strange,' he thought again. The little cook with the ladle could not possibly be the Boss.

He thought hard. The microphone simply must be in the galley. Perhaps the Boss had thrown the cook out for a minute or two, given his orders through the hidden microphone, and then disappeared again.

But this was hardly likely. He frowned. His mind raced. Perhaps, after all, the microphone was installed somewhere else? But where? He simply must find out where the Boss was, and who he was. Only when he knew the identity of his opponent could he seriously think of taking up arms against a crook who was acknowledged a Master in the World of Crime.

Suddenly three men approached in solemn procession. They were carrying about thirty large plates and spoons, and they were evidently on their way to the after-cabin. It was 19.35. In just over half an hour supper should be served.

'Got it!' he thought as he saw the men with the plates and spoons. 'Now I know how to unmask the Boss!' The hungry looks on their faces gave him the idea. He metaphorically rubbed his hands with glee at the thought of the ingenious plan he had just devised.

Several sailors were loitering near the galley.

'I'm starving,' said one of them. 'I haven't had anything to eat for over an hour.

'The sea air takes it out of you,' said another.

Altogether some fifteen sailors were standing about in small groups, and they all seemed to be very hungry. They kept looking at their watches, they kept looking at the seagulls and at each other; and they kept guessing what the Boss would serve up for supper.

By 20.00 hours more than twenty-five men were queueing up outside the after-cabin. The time had come for Agaton Sax to strike. He would use his own deadly secret weapon: the soup.

Unnoticed he crept cautiously to the back door of the galley, opened it, and slipped in. The huge stock-pot was steaming on the stove. The little fellow in the chef's tall hat turned round with a friendly smile as he heard Agaton Sax open the door.

'Would you like a piece of chocolate?' Agaton Sax said in his most ingratiating voice.

The cook took a piece from the fine box Agaton Sax offered, and bit it with relish. After a few seconds he gave a huge yawn, stretched his arms above his head, and said sleepily:

'Wish I was a there bed galley this in, that so could take a I nap little.'

'But there is a bed,' Agaton Sax said, taking him by the hand.

'Is there, there is?' the cook said, yawning again. 'You thank uncle, night-good and!'

Agaton Sax led him swiftly down a narrow staircase to a small cabin below the galley, where the little chap immediately fell asleep. Then he hurried back to the galley, fitted a rubber tube to the tap of the stock-pot and drained the thick soup into the sink. From there it flowed out into the blue water of the Channel.

He left the galley by the back door, and walked slowly towards the after-cabin. Almost the whole crew was assembled there. It was 20.30. A good deal of hungry

grumbling and protesting could be heard. As time went on, the mumblings of discontent increased in volume and intensity. At 20.45 there was open revolt.

'Is where supper?'

'Is where cook the?'

'I'm not starving to death on this damned ship.'

'How can you strike the Blow of the Century if you don't get anything to eat?'

'Gobbled cook up the has supper the himself all by!'

'If there is a cook!'

'If there is a supper!'

'We'd better see what's happening before it's too late.'

The captain came on the scene, his furious face as red as his hair.

'What's all this about?' he roared.

'Supper,' replied several of the men threateningly.

'What about supper?' said the captain.

'That's right—what about it?'

'What about what, you incoherent lay-abouts?'

'There is no supper yet, sir! How do we know there ever will be any?'

The captain's red hair turned a shade redder.

'P Eleven and G Eighteen—go to the kitchen and look into it.'

'Look into what, sir?'

'Into the soup—you fools!'

The two rogues hurried off. A moment later they were back, breathless with excitement.

'Soup, sir, the! Is no, sir, there soup!'

'Cook the, sir! Is no there cook, sir!'

For a few seconds silence hung over the men gathered on the deck. Ominously, like stormy petrels gliding overhead, the terrible words hovered in the air.

'There is no soup! There is no cook!'

The dread tidings echoed from port to starboard, from stem to stern, the cry rang out from mast to mast, and reverberated through the rigging, until, at last, it reached the ears of Archibald Duck, who was still scanning the horizon through his long telescope. He lowered it, and, frowning thoughtfully, remarked:

'There seems to be a certain restlessness on board. I don't like it. What's going on?'

A noise like the roar of an angry football crowd rose

from the after-cabin. The whole crew was bearing down on the galley. The captain bellowed, waved his fists in the air, and tore at his flaming hair in frantic rage. But the crew were angry too. Inexorably they surged on towards the galley. Five men pushed in (five others got stuck in the doorway). Almost at once those outside heard wild shouts:

'The pot is empty!'

'The cook has scoffed the lot!'

'Mutiny!'

'Throw the captain overboard!'

'Over the side with him!'

'Bully!'

'Tyrant!'

Agaton Sax followed every act of this thrilling drama with considerable satisfaction. His plan, a very simple one, had worked perfectly. When he poured out the soup his intention had been to rouse such a fury in the crew that only the Boss himself could quell the riot. In this way, and in this way only could he force the Boss to reveal himself.

Now, at last, Agaton Sax saw his deadly enemy! An insignificant man of medium height appeared on deck and walked warily towards the galley. He looked just like the rest of the crew—which was, of course, exactly what he intended. He edged through a little door at the back of the galley. So that was the hide-out where the microphone was concealed.

Agaton Sax pressed close up against the wall. The angry voices buzzed louder than ever.

Then the familiar, cold voice came through the loud-speaker:

'Friends! Rogues! Highwaymen! Lend me your ears! This is the Boss! Silent not who is he, silenced be will!'

There was a deathly hush, as one might expect after such a proclamation. The Boss spoke again:

'The cook has disappeared. Some infamous traitor has thrown away our soup. We shall hunt him down and punish him. You will have fresh soup in twenty minutes if you come back to the after-cabin. I want the captain in the galley. Now!'

Agaton Sax crept round the corner to the little door at the back of the galley. The crew, so wild a few moments ago, were now as docile as a flock of sheep. The captain hurried to the Boss; Agaton Sax heard his voice again, this time speaking to the captain:

'The what devil mean you do letting by traitor invisible an away soup the throw?'

'Sir, seen invisible have any traitor not I,' the captain answered quite truthfully.

'About the what cook? Happened to what him has?'

'Couldn't sir, be that I know expected to, sir.'

'Couldn't couldn't you, you? You are the captain,

remember! Find him immediately—and I'll find the invisible traitor. And have some soup brewed in twenty minutes, or I'll . . .'

'Sir, right!'

The captain dashed off, trembling in every limb. Two minutes later the Boss slipped out of his secret headquarters and strolled across the deck to mix with the rest of the crew who, of course, had no idea who he was.

Agaton Sax made a detour, so as to approach the Boss who was now chatting with three other men, without causing suspicion. He could not help admiring the Boss's wonderful skill in acting a part. He had just become an ordinary member of his own crew. 'He is amazing. Almost as clever as I am,' Agaton Sax mused.

But how could the Boss ever hope to outwit the ace-detective? Agaton Sax now had the advantage he had schemed for so patiently. Over and over again the Boss glanced round anxiously. He must have inspiration to solve the mystery that was tormenting him: who was outmanœuvring him at every turn? Who was the traitor in their midst? What masterly mind had planned the raid on the soup, a blow directed against the Boss himself?

But after each glance, each searching look at the rogues idling on the deck, he had to admit that the mystery was as impenetrable as ever. Once he looked straight at Agaton Sax. But the ace-detective played his part so well that the Boss didn't give him a second thought. After all, he couldn't be sure that Agaton Sax, his most terrible enemy, had a finger in this pie at all. The Boss and his crew were certainly in the soup!

12

Pirates on the port bow

The sun had gone down into the sea, and darkness had fallen. The *Esmeralda*'s bows cut through the waves at a steady eight knots. The wind moaned softly in the rigging and the starry heavens arched above the beautiful ship. The crew had had their soup and were content.

Only four men remained on duty, the others were sleeping the sleep of the unjust.

A small, dark figure suddenly emerged from the darkness, and approached the man at the helm, whose plump hands had a firm grip on the wheel.

'Am third the mate I,' the dark figure said. 'All everything right is?'

'Aye, sir, aye,' the helmsman answered. 'Everything O is K.'

'I need a hand,' said the third mate—no other than Agaton Sax. 'Can you spare anyone?'

'Aye, aye, sir. You can take Sycamore Flint. He's over there on the windward side.'

'Sycamore Flint's no good to me, he's too stupid.'

'Right you are, sir. Then take B Six, he's over on the leeward side, he's got some sense, sir.'

Agaton Sax went across to B Six.

'Orders,' he said.

'Aye, aye, sir.'

The man got up, and followed Agaton Sax to a pile of spare booms, behind which the loudspeaker was hidden.

'Help me shift these, will you?' said Agaton Sax.

'Yes, sir. Is this the gadget you want to move, sir?' B Six said, pointing to the loudspeaker.

'No, not the loudspeaker, the cable. The Boss wants it moved.'

'Very good, sir. I'm used to moving, sir, I've moved five times in the last few months, sir, it's a bit risky to have the same address for too long you know, sir.'

With the help of B Six Agaton Sax disconnected the cable from the microphone he had found in the little hide-out behind the galley. Then they pulled the cable below the deck and attached it once more to the microphone. But this time the microphone was in a new hiding place, that Agaton Sax had found earlier while prowling round under cover of darkness. Both cable and microphone were now absolutely invisible from the deck.

'That's it,' said Agaton Sax, pleased with his night's work. 'Have a piece of chocolate. Take two, if you like, you must be pretty hungry.'

B Six took two pieces. Three minutes later he yawned. Agaton Sax watched him closely. At just the right moment he took his hand and led him down to an empty cabin.

'Good night to you, sir—good night, sir Uncle, I mean,' B Six said, almost asleep, and stretched out on the bunk.

'Good night, old man,' Agaton Sax said kindly, 'you'll be all right in the morning.'

Now everything was ready. The decisive blow would be struck at first light. He set his micro-alarm-watch at six, and fell asleep. This watch—a wonderful invention of his own—was so small that it fitted in his left ear. When it rang no one but Agaton Sax could hear it. Five hours later the alarm went off. With a dynamic bound he leapt from his bunk, full of energy, his wonderful mind refreshed and ready for action.

There were now about ten men busy on the deck. Unnoticed, Agaton Sax slipped into the hide-out.

His heart beat a little faster than usual. He knew that this time he was playing a dangerous game, and the stakes were high.

From his hide-out he could see the greater part of the deck without being seen himself. He picked up the microphone and slowly put it to his lips. The moment had come.

Then, just as he was about to speak, something totally unexpected happened—something so unreal and so fantastic that it would have silenced him, even if he had already started to speak. He stood dumbfounded, staring in front of him.

What was going on? Was he dreaming? No—for now he heard it again—for the second time he heard the incredible words which had struck him dumb a moment ago:

'Pirate ship sighted on the port bow! I repeat—pirate ship sighted!'

The speaker was the ship's owner himself, Mr Archibald Duck. He had remained on watch all night, standing in the crow's nest, at attention and resolute, unfailingly true to his own ideal of seamanship and naval gallantry. He pressed his magnificent telescope to his right eye, and his face was grim, stern and determined. He was

aware of his duty, and of his responsibility as supreme commander on board.

'Mr Duck must be dreaming—he has been awake all night—he must be talking in his sleep—or he is just dotty—yes, he must be off his nut—I have suspected it all along,' Agaton Sax thought. He rubbed his chin, not without alarm. 'Damn it, he is spoiling my brilliant plan!'

Cautiously he crept from his hiding place. A crowd of bewildered sailors had gathered on deck. Archibald Duck stood motionless as ever. He shouted:

'She's flying the Jolly Roger! She's bearing straight down on us!'

Agaton Sax stared. His eyes wide with astonishment. He could not believe it. And yet—there she was—a glorious brig with dazzling white sails—the spray flying about her bows—the sea-gulls wheeling above her mast-heads. Agaton Sax pulled out his pocket telescope. Unbelievable! Incredible! Archibald Duck was not delirious! From the top of the brig's main mast the terrifying black flag with its skull and crossbones streamed in the wind! It was a pirate ship, and there was no mistake about her course—she was heading straight for the *Esmeralda*—already he could see the pirates moving about her deck, eager for their prey, running their fingers along the blades of their cutlasses and throwing hungry glances at the magnificent ship they were about to board and loot.

Agaton Sax went back to his hide-out. He mopped his forehead. All kinds of thoughts flashed across his mind. What did this mean? How could such a thing happen? There had been no piracy for a hundred and fifty years.

Then, suddenly, he understood. And as soon as he understood, he knew what he had to do.

He picked up the microphone again, and switched it on. Then, speaking in perfect imitation of the Boss's voice, he addressed the crew.

'Attention, all of you! This is the Boss speaking! There are no pirates! I repeat: No pirates are at large in this civilised age. Law and order rule the seas. Don't be afraid! These are only fancy-dress pirates, and they are our friends. Their captain is the famous French gang leader Bouchardieu de Clignancourt, and he and I have business to do. As a matter of fact, he's the one man who can interpret the Register. He's worth millions to us! Treat him well! He and his chief advisers are coming on board so that we can negotiate terms.'

As Agaton Sax finished speaking he peered out through a little hole in the wall. The crew had assembled on the windward side, to listen to the voice from the loud speaker, which they believed was the Boss's. They were watching the pirate ship closely as it bore swiftly down on them.

Agaton Sax turned his attention to the Boss, who was standing with Belisarius Mock and Sycamore Flint. It was very difficult to describe exactly the colour of his face as he listened to the false voice coming from the loud-speaker, but a skilled painter might have contrived something between sulphur yellow, a dirty brick red, and apoplectic lilac. But the uncertainty of mind that produced this strange change of colour lasted only for a moment. Then, drawing his revolver, he bounded, panther-like into the galley. Seeing that the microphone was no longer there, he dashed out. Bewildered, he hesitated, looking her and there; then he ran to the gunwale, threw a quick glance up into the rigging where he caught sight of Archibald Duck. He paused, and it seemed for a moment as if he thought it was Duck who had imitated his voice. Then with a shake of his head he dismissed that suspicion as impossible, and made a dive for the loudspeaker. He followed the cable in a desperate attempt to find the hidden microphone, but almost at once it disappeared under the deck, and he realised he could no longer follow it. Now his face began to change colour again. Angry though he was, he never forgot to behave as unobtrusively as possible; because it was still vital that he should not reveal his true identity to the rest of the crew.

Agaton Sax waited in his hide-out. He was absolutely calm, and a smile of satisfaction played round his mouth as he watched the Boss's desperate and furious efforts to find the man who, by imitating his voice, could destroy his leadership.

'The game is up, my friend,' Agaton Sax murmured to himself.

But at that very moment something happened which upset his plans entirely. It happened so suddenly that even he was disconcerted.

From the pirate ship a cannon-shot was fired.

The explosion was deafening. The wretched crew threw themselves to the side of the ship and ducked behind the gunwale, where they held their hands to their ears, trembling in every limb.

There was another cannon-shot, another roar as stunning as the first. Smoke belched forth from the cannon on board the pirate ship, whose name, *Black Hawk*, could now be seen, painted on her bows, and whose wild crew were executing an exuberant war-dance on the main deck.

Agaton Sax started. For one terrible moment he felt bewildered and uneasy. But his wonderfully efficient brain came to the rescue and he regained command of himself almost at once. He was confident he could handle this emergency.

Through his peep-hole he saw the pirate captain standing on the brig's gunwale, a black patch over his left eye and an enormous sabre in his right hand. He flourished his sabre and called out:

'Ready for boarding!'

A tremendous cheer went up from the pirate crew, who brandished sabres, daggers and blunderbusses. The *Esmeralda*'s crew, on the other hand, crouched paralysed behind the gunwale.

Agaton Sax switched on the microphone. This time he had an even more felicitous plan. He spoke once more in the Boss's cold voice:

'Listen all of you! This is the Boss speaking. The voice you heard a few minutes ago was that of a traitor, a crook, an unscrupulous rogue, our common enemy, Agaton Sax! Once more he has sneaked into our midst! He stole the hidden microphone, and imitated my voice in order to drive you all to destruction. It was he who poured away your soup and now he intends to hand you over to the pirates. For they are pirates—they are not our friends, as he told you. This is the Boss speaking, I repeat, this is the Boss speaking. Listen carefully! This scoundrel Agaton Sax is none other than B Eight! Seize B Eight at once—he is Agaton Sax in disguise! Do you understand? He is between Sycamore Flint and Belisarius Mock. Can you see him? Good! That man is Agaton Sax—our mortal enemy! Arrest him, and hand him over to the pirates! He's the man they are after—not you!

They will reward you with fifty-thousand pounds when you deliver him to them!'

Agaton Sax finished speaking, and watched calmly while the expected happened. B Eight—that is, the Boss—leaped in the air as if he had been bitten by a

snake—a reaction that was the best possible proof of his guilt. The rogues had no doubt he was Agaton Sax, their mortal enemy, and before he had time to convince them that he was not he was seized by seven pairs of strong, brawny arms, and trussed like a chicken, with some seventy feet of good, strong rope wound round his body. Wrapped up like an Egyptian Mummy, he was hoisted on to the bulwark and shown in triumph to the pirates whose ship was now so close that the crews could speak to each other.

'Here he is, here's Agaton Sax, the traitor!' the rogues shouted. 'He's all yours.'

The pirate captain lifted his sabre above his head. Behind him thronged his band of wild pirates. Some had patches over their eyes, some had wooden legs, they were armed with grapples, boarding axes, sabres, pistols, rifles, daggers, and so forth. Almost paralysed with terror, the rogues on board the *Esmeralda* held the Boss aloft, and waved him slowly, just as soldiers wave a white flag of truce when they want to parley with the enemy.

But to their dismay, the pirate captain brandished his sabre wildly, roaring:

'Defend yourselves!'

His whole crew pressed behind him, flourishing their strange weapons and echoing his words.

'Defend yourselves! Put up a fight. Scum of the sea! Forward!'

The crew stood as if hypnotised, still waving the swathed body of the Boss back and forth. Then Belisarius Mock stammered plaintively:

'But we've got him here! Can't you see him? The master-crook and swindler Agaton Sax is yours, gentlemen! We even parcelled him up for you!'

The pirate captain gaped. Then his astonishment turned to anger. With a swift gesture of fury he rounded on the pirates milling at his back, and roared:

'What the devil's going on? Who's playing the lead here? Is it me or is it that coil of rope they call Atom

Slacks? This is outrageous! By my skull and crossbones, let me speak to the Managing Director at once.'

On hearing the pirate captain's enigmatic words, a fat, red-faced gentleman pushed his way through the crowd of pirates. He was wearing a yellow straw hat and had a

black cigar in his mouth, and he was just as furious as the pirate captain. He took the cigar out of his mouth and shouted:

'You blundering fools! That's the wrong ship! Can't you see its called the *Esmeralda*? The ship we're after is the *Beatrice*—can't you even tell one woman's name from another? And what's that ridiculous parcel they're waving—is it an Egyptian mummy?'

'It seems to be someone they call Atom Slacks,' said the captain, who, still unable to penetrate the mystery removed the black patch from his eye in order to see better.

Agaton Sax thought it was high time for him to intervene. With a monkey leap he swung himself up into the shrouds, and, raising his hand, called for silence.

'Gentlemen! May I have your attention, please! I am Agaton Sax the ace-detective! The man you have wrapped up is one of the most dangerous criminals of the century, whom I have just trapped. He stole the Great Code Register of Current Criminals from Scotland Yard, and manned this ship with a crew of forty villains, trained by himself. May I suggest that you, the crew of the *Black Hawk*, arrest the lot. All except for the owner of the ship, Archibald Duck, the multi-millionaire, who is certainly not a member of the gang. He is at his look-out post in the crow's nest and you must not take him into custody.'

Archibald Duck, who had been watching Agaton Sax through his spy-glass started as he heard these words and his face was suddenly lit by a radiant smile.

'Are you really Agaton Sax, the ace-detective? If so my happiness is complete!'

Exhausted by the dramatic events of the last half hour, the Boss's wretched gang surrendered to the crew of the *Black Hawk*. Their hands were bound, they were taken below decks and given warm soup. Only the Boss was still left, parcelled, on the deck of the *Esmeralda*.

Agaton Sax, his manner calm and dignified, boarded the *Black Hawk*, and introduced himself to the man in the straw-hat, who turned out to be none other than

Buck Hopp, the famous film producer, internationally acclaimed for his magnificent historical films. Mr Hopp read the document Agaton Sax handed to him—Lispington's letter confirming Agaton Sax's identity and right to arrest. Mr Hopp took the cigar out of his mouth and looked at Agaton Sax with interest and respect.

'It has been a great honour for us to be able to assist you in apprehending these dangerous criminals,' he said, removing his straw hat as an even greater sign of respect. 'The only thing that worries me now is what has happened to the *Beatrice*. You haven't by any chance seen a three-masted barque of that name have you, Mr Sax?'

'Indeed I have,' said Agaton Sax. 'There!'

He pointed to the horizon, and there she was—another glorious ship, heading straight for the *Esmeralda* and the *Black Hawk*.

'You will understand, Mr Sax, that our attack on your ship was a regrettable mistake,' Mr Hopp went on. 'My company is engaged in shooting a wonderful new production in vista-breadth-width-length-stereo-chromo-colour-vision. I beseech you not to miss it when it comes your way. To make sure I'll see you get two free tickets. It will be called *Black Patch—The Terror of the Seven Seas*. Yesterday and to-day we intended to shoot a great sea battle between the *Black Hawk* and the *Beatrice*. But unfortunately we lost sight of the *Beatrice* just after sunset last night, and when we sighted your ship, naturally we thought that you were the missing *Beatrice*. My actors eagerly resumed their roles, we fired a couple of blanks across your bows, the cameras started up, your sailors retaliated in just the way we planned; everything was perfect. Then, judge for yourself, Mr Sax, what a cruel and mystifying blow it was to us when your crew suddenly surrendered in the most cowardly and unseamanlike manner, and our glorious sea-fight was ruined.'

Agaton Sax nodded sympathetically. Then he crossed over to the *Esmeralda*. The Boss lay on the deck. He looked at Agaton Sax with eyes that burned with hatred.

For a moment the two men stared at each other. Then Agaton Sax spoke, and his words caused Mr Buck Hopp to wonder whether he was dreaming:

'Fate you your met in soup the spilt!'

With a gentlemanly bow Agaton Sax left the Boss, who was then hustled below decks, to be handed over later to Scotland Yard.

Agaton Sax explained to Mr Duck and Mr Hopp that the Boss and his gang had volunteered to crew the *Esmeralda* in order to slip quietly away from England without attracting the attention of Scotland Yard. The

Boss had intended to overpower Mr Duck in the Channel, and then sail the *Esmeralda* to France, where he had arranged to meet the greatest of all French gangsters, Bouchardieu de Clignancourt, the only man in the world, except Agaton Sax, who could read the Criminal Register without the Key.

There is little more to tell. The fourteen boxes containing the Register were transported in triumph to Scotland Yard. Lispington was transported too, but in his case, with joy. Agaton Sax caught Bouchardieu de Clignancourt three days later. Archibald Duck was offered a minor part in the film—and earned some money for the first time in his life.

Finally, Old Goat Beard—the genuine one—embraced Agaton Sax with southern fervour, exclaiming:

'Gotobarbarossorokontorontan h'p Agaton, dutchoglossophonèpromo Sax dublolinguaparlamentaristara he, Mr?'

Those words mean, of course: 'By the hairs of my beard, Mr Agaton Sax, how on earth did you master such a difficult language as Scramble-talk?'

If you enjoyed this book and would like to have information sent you about other TARGET titles, write to the address below.

You will also receive:

A FREE TARGET BADGE!

Based on the TARGET BOOKS symbol—see front cover of this book—this attractive three-colour badge, pinned to your blazer-lapel, or jumper, will excite the interest and comment of all your friends!

and you will be further entitled to:

FREE ENTRY INTO THE TARGET DRAW!

All you have to do is cut off the coupon beneath, write on it your name and address *in block capitals*, and pin it to your letter. You will be advised of your lucky draw number. Twice a year, in June and December, numbers will be drawn 'from the hat' and the winner will receive a complete year's set of TARGET books.

Write to: TARGET BOOKS,
Universal-Tandem Publishing Co.,
14 Gloucester Road,
London SW7 4RD

——————————— cut here ———————————

Full name...

Address...

....

..............................County......................................

Age..............................